David Alex Jones

ANGELA'S EYES

The Survivor Trilogy:
Prequel

This is a work of fiction. Names, characters, places, and incidents are either the product of the author's imagination, or are used fictitiously. Any resemblance to actual events, locales, or persons, living or dead, is purely coincidental.

Cover Art by David Alex Jones

Published by:
Apparently Normal Publishing
Waterloo, Ontario, Canada

ISBN (Paperback Edition) 978-0-9948796-5-3
Version 2023.01.01

LAND ACKNOWLEDGEMENT

This book was written in Southwestern Ontario, Canada, on land located within the Haldimand Tract, land that was granted to the Haudenosaunee of the Six Nations of the Grand River, and is within the shared traditional territory of the Neutral, Anishinaabe, and Haudenosaunee peoples

TABLE OF CONTENTS

Foreword i

Prologue 1

Chapter 1 7

Chapter 2 17

Chapter 3 35

Chapter 4 57

Chapter 5 71

Chapter 6 87

Chapter 7 103

Chapter 8 126

Chapter 9 145

Chapter 10 164

Chapter 11 181

Chapter 12 200

Chapter 13 220

Chapter 14 231

Acknowledgements 247

Other Books by David Alex Jones 249

About the Author 250

Excerpt: Faces 251

Excerpt: Walls 263

FOREWORD

While I was outlining the story for *Faces*, the second novel in *The Survivor Trilogy*, so many good ideas emerged for the character of Angela Baranyi that there just wasn't enough room in *Faces* to tell all of Angela's story. With three distinct subplots in *Faces*, it was a difficult enough task for me to keep that story moving along, and I didn't want to risk losing my readers by making the story any more complex than it already was. And yet, it seemed like Angela's story was compelling by itself, just begging to be told. The solution to my dilemma became obvious. I realized that I had enough material to have Angela tell her own story from a first person perspective. So, I wrote *Angela's Eyes* as a companion novella—a Prequel—to complement *Faces*.

You might ask, "Should I read *Angela's Eyes* before or after I read *Faces*?"

I think either option works just as well. Angela's story flows naturally from the Epilogue of the first book in the Trilogy, *Walls*, so it fits well if read between *Walls* and *Faces*. On the other hand, Julia Gibbs who proof-read *Faces* before she read

Angela's Eyes, enjoyed finding out more about Angela *after* she had already read *Faces*. So in the end, it's your choice whether you choose to read this book before or after you read *Faces*. Either way, it gives much more depth, not only to Angela's character, but it also does the same for the character of Pastor Soren Kristiansen, the villain in *Faces*.

Finally, the idea for having a character venture into the Las Vegas floodway system came to me after seeing a brief TV news clip about the huge increase in homeless people taking refuge in the tunnels beneath Las Vegas after the economic crash of 2011. As I researched the topic further I came upon an eye opening book on the subject by Matthew O'Brien, with photographs by Danny Mollohan and cover photograph by Bill Hughes. The vivid descriptions contained within the pages of that book, of another dark, subterranean existence beneath the sparkle and glamour of the Las Vegas Strip, were instrumental in imagining how and why a fictional character would find his or her way into the tunnels, and what it would be like to try to survive there.

Reference.
O'Brien, Matthew. Beneath the Neon: Life and Death in the Tunnels of Las Vegas. Huntington Press, Las Vegas, NV. 2007.

PROLOGUE

I REMEMBER that day, almost one year ago, like it was yesterday. My eyes were wide open and alert to my surroundings, as they had been every day since I stole 4.7 million dollars from Soren Kristiansen and went on the run, vanishing from the lives of everybody I knew and loved. From that day on, my eyes have kept a constant vigil. I've been paranoid about every person I see, unable to trust a soul and waiting for the day when Soren eventually finds me.

The setting sun was disappearing behind the towering landscape of downtown Los Angeles, the daytime heat giving way to long, late afternoon shadows. I sat on the grass in the San Julian Park, leaning up against a cinderblock wall, trying to blend into the shadows. This had become my usual afternoon and evening routine — hiding in plain sight in this small green oasis amidst the most unfortunate of humanity. As usual, the park was crowded with people; leaning up against trees, lying on the grass, or sitting cross-legged on the ground. In the park and out on the street, throngs of other street-people staked their claim to a small square of sidewalk or grass to set up temporary sleeping quarters for the coming night. They unpacked portable tents or cardboard boxes from the shopping carts that contained the sum total of their possessions. The small mass of humanity in East Los Angeles was winding down another day of subsistence survival in the unseen underbelly of America.

Many of the park's residents knew each other well, jabbering casually with each other. I knew many of them by sight, as they knew me. But I rarely allowed myself anything more than raising my eyebrows in acknowledgement, or a curt greeting to any of them. I wasn't willing to risk conversation or the possibility of revealing anything about myself to anybody.

I liked San Julian Park. It was a place where I could sit in the shade when it was warm, or find some sunshine when it was cool. I could keep my back to the cinderblock wall or the trunk of a tree, where I could keep a wary eye on every person who passed or entered the park. I blended in well, wearing the same pair of torn jeans, threadbare t-shirt, hoodie, and well-worn boots that I wore each time I visited the park. My shoulder-length blonde hair was purposely tousled and unkempt, and there wasn't a trace of makeup on my face. On that spring day, I wasn't wearing the grey hoodie I'd been wearing through the cooler winter months, but

I was glad I still had it with me, using it to cushion my behind from the hard ground.

I first noticed the woman with the camera while she worked her way down the opposite side of the street. I'd never seen her in the area before, so she aroused my attention immediately. She had an old-school SLR with a large telephoto lens attached, and she appeared to be taking candid photographs of people from a distance. The hairs on the back of my neck tingled. I riveted my eyes on her as she moved slowly towards the park.

The residents of Skid Row were used to seeing photojournalists who sometimes ventured here to document their existence. But this woman was different. She spent more time composing and taking each shot, manually focusing and setting the shutter speed and aperture for each exposure. She was completely engrossed, but relaxed at the same time. She was doing this for art and her own relaxation.

She was tall and thin, with an olive complexion and short dark hair. As I studied her carefully, she looked down at the SLR and checked its settings. Apparently satisfied, she raised her head and started surveying the area for potential targets. She noticed San Julian Park and started moving in my direction. I reached beneath me for my hoodie, wondering if I would be less noticeable if I pulled the hood over my head.

I decided against doing anything to attract attention, averting my eyes and hoping she wouldn't see me. It was time to leave the park. I stole a quick glance in my peripheral vision, hoping to see that her camera was focused on other residents of the park.

It was too late. I felt fear take control over my body. Instead of getting up and running, I froze. She had already spotted me and our eyes met. Automatically, she raised the camera and focused the large lens on me. Before I could look away, I saw the camera's shutter opening and closing, capturing on film the fear and distrust on my face and in my eyes. It was all over in a couple of seconds. She lowered the camera away from her face and our eyes met. She could tell that I was different from the other residents of the park — she knew I didn't belong here. If I stayed where I was any longer, I knew she was going to come closer to start asking questions.

It was time to go. I reached for the used plastic grocery bag full of personal belongings beside me, and rose quickly to my feet. I pulled the hoodie over my head and lowered my eyes, walking briskly past the mystery woman and onto the asphalt pathway that led to the park's only exit at the corner of the green space. I turned right and quickly crossed St. Julian Street. Once across the street, I hunched down and slid behind a large blue dome-tent — somebody's lodging for the night. Shielding myself from the woman's view, I moved quickly along East 5th Street, leaving the park and the woman behind.

Now, hiding from the world in my makeshift bed in the darkness of a Las Vegas floodway, I recall the ominous feeling I'd had about those photos. Somehow, I knew they were going to come back to haunt me. I didn't know when or how, but I knew the day would come. I couldn't risk having anybody seeing them. As far as the rest of the world was concerned, I was dead. I walked away from everything — my two kids and my parents — and I *ran* away from my job. As far as anybody was concerned, I had simply vanished from the face of the earth.

My premonition came true three weeks ago. Suddenly seeing my face in the background of a TV news report took me by surprise, but it wasn't a total shock. I recognized the look of fear and distrust in my eyes in the candid portrait. The same feeling of fear swept through my body as I realized the implications of what I saw. With one quick glimpse of myself on TV, my entire world had turned upside down.

Since that day, my mind has been spinning — continually replaying the events from eighteen months earlier. Could I have done anything differently? How did I, Angela Baranyi, an innocent, religious, hard-working single mother of two, ever manage to get involved in Soren Kristiansen's web of dishonesty, deceit, and crime? How did I become a criminal myself? No matter how many times I analyze the events in my mind, I haven't come up with any good answers to those questions. But the events keep replaying in my memory, like a nightmare that never ends…

CHAPTER 1

THE ROAD I've travelled — from being an honest, hard-working single mother of two children, to hiding on the streets of Los Angeles, and then in the floodways of Las Vegas — is a strange one. On one hand, I could say that it happened so quickly that I'm still in a state of shock. But when I think about it, my journey down that road really started many years ago.

My parents fled Hungary after the failed revolt in November 1956, finally settling in Cleveland's large Hungarian community. My two older sisters were born shortly after Momma and Papa's arrival in America, but I'm six years younger than my middle sister. I always felt like I was an outsider in my family. And even though there were many other children of Hungarian descent in my school, I still felt like I didn't belong. I was shy, and I've only ever had one close friend in Cleveland; Dori Sarkozy.

Looking back, I'd say that I've always been a book nerd. I've always done extremely well in school, which might explain why I never felt like I belonged with the rest of my classmates. It's the single area of my life where I've always felt confident. My parents are both well educated. Papa had been studying to be an accountant and Momma had been studying medicine when they fled from Hungary. They always made it clear to their three daughters that education comes first. I suppose I took their message to heart and overcompensated by losing myself in books. Don't get me wrong. They're good parents, but they're strict and unyielding in their outlook on life. I can't remember many times in my youth when we took vacations as a family or had much fun. I know Momma and Papa love me in their own way, but I can't say our family is very close emotionally. And I can't say I've ever really felt loved.

My experience with boys has been limited, and the experiences I've had aren't good. Because my sisters are both older, there were many times when Momma and Papa needed to find a sitter for me when they went out. The Farkas family next door, another good Hungarian family, had seven kids. Their oldest daughter Eva, and their son Michael, were often available and eager to make some spare cash. Unfortunately for me, nobody knew that Michael had a fondness for young girls. Nobody was any the wiser to the fact that he was fondling and petting me, or that his abuse advanced to oral sex and penetration with his fingers over a two-year period.

And of course, he threatened me.

'If you tell anybody, I'll come after you. You don't like what you've been doing with me? Well, you just wait and see what I do if you tell anybody! Nobody's going to believe you, anyway. I'll just tell them that you showed your little titties to me and asked me to touch them. Who do you think they're going to believe?'

Fortunately, I grew old enough that Momma and Papa started letting me stay home by myself if my sisters weren't home, and Michael graduated to abusing his high school dates.

I'm not saying I didn't attract a lot of attention from the boys at school. My blonde hair and creamy-white complexion always attracted the looks of every boy in my classes over the years. I've seen them staring at my chest and I've recognized the lust in their eyes. I did my best to push them away; feeling awkward from their attention, especially after my experiences with Michael. But at the same time, because I longed to feel loved by somebody, it became harder to resist the attention after puberty, and especially after I started high school.

When I met David Dvorak at the age of sixteen, he developed an immediate crush on me. I have to admit that his constant attention and the warmth of his arms made me feel wanted for the first time in my life. We started going everywhere and doing everything together.

Did I love David? Probably not. But what did I know about love? I felt wanted, and to me, that felt like love. After high school, David found work in a steel mill and asked me to marry him. I did my best to push him away, but he persisted. He encouraged me to go to college, so I followed in Papa's footsteps and studied accounting. But it was during the mid-eighties when I discovered my real passion — the world of personal computers. I knew that PC's were the future of accounting and I jumped in with both feet, first learning to write code for the crude Apple II machines, then graduating to both Macs and PC's. I was one of the first computer geeks — and most definitely one of the first female geeks.

David always wanted children, especially a son, but I never really felt comfortable with sex. I'd never told anybody about being sexually abused by Michael Farkas, not even my parents or David. And my work and my passion for the world of PC's left me with little interest in having children. So I managed to keep putting David off.

"You know I need to study hard to pass my exams," I would say. "It isn't easy working all day and coming home to study every night. When would I have time to take care of kids? Once I pass my exams, I promise we'll have kids. I'll be thirty by then, and I know I can't wait forever."

In the meantime, David spent more and more time at the bar with his buddies. After their long days in the mill, he developed an increasingly closer relationship with alcohol as the years progressed.

By the time I turned thirty, I couldn't hold David off any longer. I went off the pill and got pregnant soon afterwards. As fate would have it, the steel mill closed and David found himself unemployed. I became the sole source of income for our soon-to-be family. David became increasingly disillusioned with life and we grew more distant, even as our first child, Julia, was born in 1996. His dependence on alcohol became more obvious, and our arguing increased in frequency and intensity. David promised to dry out. To his credit, he tried to stop drinking many times. But, with few skills and little education, his job prospects weren't great. He refused to "lower himself" to work in any setting where they weren't paying the kind of wages he was making as a unionized worker in the mill. He was slamming the door on his future, and I knew it.

By then, I had started working in a small accounting firm owned by an old friend of my father. Mr. Kovacs was old-school. He consistently underestimated my talents and under-compensated me for my hard work. But I only had myself to blame. I'd always been passive and afraid to speak up for myself, especially when it came to men. David and I found ourselves struggling financially and arguing more and more about money. The final straw came when he hit me on the side of the head one night during an argument. Nicholas, our son, was only a year old and Julia was three. The writing was on the wall and I knew I had to leave. My parents were horrified that I left, but reluctantly took me, Julia, and Nicholas in. I know they secretly hoped that David and I would work things out and I'd go back to him. Momma tried to scare me into going back.

"Angela, a woman can't survive in this world by herself, especially with two young children. Think about what you're doing, dear. It can't be that bad. Go see the priest and ask for his guidance and prayers."

Momma didn't understand that David and I came from two different worlds. He carried forward the old world values where the man was expected to take care of his wife and kids, and where he wasn't considered to be much of a man if he wasn't doing his job. His self-esteem disappeared as his job prospects dried up. On the other hand, Momma and Papa had always instilled in me the drive to learn and the need to be able to support myself. David eventually resented my education and the implication that I might always be the major income earner in the family.

"It's okay, Momma," I would say. "We're two different people and it's time for me to move on. I can't take the drinking anymore. He can't change. He's tried, but he just can't stop. I can survive — just wait and see. I'll ask for a raise at work, or I'll find another job. It should only be a few months before I can afford a place for me and the kids."

The educated, professional side of me was confident about my future. But deep inside, there was a part of me that blamed myself for everything — even for the sexual abuse from Michael Farkas. And even though the educated part of me refused to acknowledge it, I blamed myself for not being a better lover and wife for David. Deep down, I didn't feel I was a good enough for anything. I didn't even feel assertive enough to ask Mr. Kovacs for a well-deserved raise.

I now recognize how helpless and worthless I really felt after the separation. I was still best friends with Dori, and I put on my brave, confident face whenever I was with her. But after the kids were in bed, I wallowed in despair and self-loathing, desperate to find something that would help me feel better. I was well-acquainted with the dangers of addiction to alcohol. So instead, I found the internet.

And very soon, I found Pastor Soren Kristiansen and the *World-Wide Community of Christ,* with his message of hopefulness and optimism. Word of his streaming internet church services and his charismatic personality had spread with viral speed. I admired his amazing confidence and his commitment to helping others. I told Dori about him. Unlike me, she had chosen the path of being a stay-at-home mom. But she also felt like she had lost touch with who she was. Like me, she was depressed and was also mesmerized by Pastor Kristiansen's charisma and his messages of hope. We were both addicted to chatting online with other followers, and we both started donating what little we could afford to the Pastor's mission work. It helped us feel better about ourselves.

IT'S FEBRUARY 2, 2003 — Groundhog Day — and I'm feeling particularly depressed at the prospect of another six weeks of winter. Julia and Nicholas are tucked in bed and I finally have some time to unwind before calling it a night. Out of habit, I click on the WWCC website. However, unlike other nights, I'm greeted by a huge banner on Pastor Soren's home page.

'See Pastor Kristiansen's Ministry — Live and In-Person!'

The banner invites me to click on a link for the dates for his live Ministry tour. I feel my hands trembling with excitement as I search the list for dates. Finally, I see what I'm looking for.

'See Pastor Kristiansen in Cleveland — Gund Arena — March 23, 2003.' My hands are still shaking, I feel my heart pounding in my chest, and I realize I've been holding my breath. I allow myself to let out a long breath. There is no way in the world I'm going to miss this!

Having barely slept after my discovery, I phone Dori the next morning to share my excitement with her. It doesn't take any time at all to convince her to come with me to see Pastor Soren's Ministry.

"Pastor Kristiansen?… Coming to Cleveland?… You're kidding?… Of course I'll go with you!… I can't believe he's coming here; he's so hot!"

Dori blurts her secret. She harbors a gigantic crush for the good Pastor. But, unlike Dori, my attraction to Pastor Soren isn't sexual. I'm hooked on chatting online with other believers, on devoting my life to God, and on committing myself to Pastor Kristiansen's missions to help others. It makes me feel good about myself. And for the first time in my life, it makes me feel like I know where I belong.

I book our tickets to Pastor Soren's Ministry over my lunch hour. I feel excited and hopeful for the first time in months. I manage to tap into the self-confidence of my professional side, which has been missing for many months. For the time being,

I manage to block out the self-blame and guilt that has plagued me since leaving David.

Not only do I find my missing self-confidence, but I begin to feel downright bold. I'm not going to be content with just seeing Pastor Kristiansen from a distance. My heart is pumping and my hands are trembling again as I click on a button to enter a contest — a chance to meet our idol in person at the conclusion of the March 23 event.

I've found my mojo and I feel like I'm on the road to recovery… or so I think.

CHAPTER 2

THE MORNING of March 23, 2003 comes far too early. My eyes pop open and I turn my head to look at the alarm clock — four-thirty, and I can't get back to sleep. Excitement is pulsing through my body. The long-awaited day has finally arrived. Dori and I are finally going to see Pastor Soren Kristiansen in person tonight.

A flood of conflicting emotions surges through my body — excitement at being able to see my idol, mixed with disappointment. I didn't win the contest, and I won't be meeting Pastor Soren in person. But we still have one last chance to see him up close. The event is festival seating, so we need to line up in front of the Gund Arena early to get the best possible seats.

On the way to the shower, I pick up the phone and dial Dori's house.

"Are you awake?" I ask, my voice full of excitement.

"I am now," Dori answers, her voice still croaky.

"Just giving you your wake-up call, like you asked," I say. "I'll have a quick shower and be at your place by five-thirty. Make sure you dress warm. Bring your chair and blanket. It's still March, you know."

"Yeah, I know. I'll be ready. See you later, sunshine," she says. I detect a note of sarcasm in her voice.

Hurriedly, I wash my hair and lather the rest of my body in record time. I turn on the hairdryer, tossing my wavy blonde hair so the hot air can work its magic. I realize there's no way it's going to be completely dry in time, so I settle for the *au naturel* wet look. My mind is racing.

What am I going to wear? I'm going to church, but it's not really a church service — it's more like a celebration. In the website photos, everybody seems to be casually dressed for Pastor Soren's events. But I don't want to look like a slob, either. I may have to wait outside in the cold, but I want to look nice during the ministry.

I come to the conclusion that there is no single solution to my dilemma. I'm going to have to do a makeover at the arena. I quickly throw on clean panties and a bra while I decide what to wear. Then I grab my newest pair of blue jeans and a heavy sweater from my bureau and quickly pull them on. That will do for standing in line outside. I open my closet, removing the new spring dress I bought last weekend. Standing in front of the mirror, I admire it and I hold it up against my body.

The grey print against a cream background is subtle and classy. The high neckline and knee-length is professional enough for work, but still looks casual. I like the way the belted waist makes me look slim. I'm not sure why it seems so important, but somehow I feel like I need to make a good impression. I leave it on the hanger for now. I find my best pair of black high-heeled shoes and drop them into a gym bag, along with some makeup for touch-ups later on. As I run out of my room, I remember to pick out a light sweater to wear over the dress, in case the arena is cool, and I put it in the bag as well.

On my way out, I look in on Julia and Nicholas, still sound asleep in their beds. Careful not to waken anybody, I tiptoe downstairs, quickly make a thermos of instant hot chocolate and pick up the snacks I'd set out the night before, depositing them in the gym bag. My blanket and fold-out chair are already packed in the hatch of my old Hyundai. I step into my ankle-high brown leather boots and zip them up the side, then I don my woolen winter coat, gloves, and toque. The forecast is for temperatures in the low thirties. It's going to be a long, cold wait.

After hanging my dress inside the car and scraping the frost from my windshield, I head for Dori's place, finding her waiting in the doorway for me. As she emerges from her house and closes the door quietly behind her, she turns and flashes a gigantic smile.

"Can you believe it's finally here? I thought this day would never come!" she squeals.

"Me too," I sigh. "Now we just have to keep from freezing to death while we wait in line."

THERE ARE about thirty people already in line by the time we park the Hyundai and make our way to the Gund Arena's main entrance. Wristbands are distributed as soon as we arrive, to ensure that we're rewarded for our frigid ordeal. The mood in the line-up is one of celebration. Everybody in the line-up is energized for the big event, and many pass the time reading Bible passages, praying, or singing.

Dori and I take turns using the car to go for hot food and drinks, and to use a warm restroom rather than a cold porta-pot. We join in with a group near us who are singing hymns, feeling the anticipation and excitement building inside us as the day progresses.

Finally, at five p.m., two hours before the event is to begin, the front doors open and we make a mad dash into the arena. We race down a flight of stairs to the arena floor, then sprint to the front of the arena, managing to snare a couple of seats in the front row, to the right side of center. Dori and I jump up and down frantically, hugging each other, intoxicated with the knowledge that we are finally going to fulfil our dream of seeing Pastor Soren close-up.

Once we eventually calm down, I make my way to the Women's room before it gets too congested. I change into the dress, high heels, and light sweater, then spend some time in front of the mirror, adding some makeup. Eventually, I feel like my face matches with how good I look in my dress. I nod my approval, pack my jeans, sneakers, and heavy sweater in the gym bag, and I make my way back to our front-row seats.

For the next hour and a half, we celebrate spontaneously with the crowd around us, singing songs and chanting for Pastor Soren. After a while, I notice some roadies onstage. They're running around, checking connections, and looking flustered. They're shouting into hand-held radios, their faces etched with worried frowns. I notice them gathering at the sound booth at the back of the arena. It's obvious that they're having some kind technical difficulties. The geek in me can't help it — my curiosity gets the best of me.

"I'm going for a walk to stretch my legs," I say to Dori. I head towards the back of the arena, slowing as I approach the sound booth, trying to overhear what they are saying.

"Damn!" one man curses. "I knew we shouldn't 'a switched to computers to run the show. At least with the ol' boards we knew how'ta trouble-shoot."

"We've got a backup, don't we?" asks a second man.

"No, this *is* the damn backup!" the first man answers. "I was havin' trouble with the first computer, an' this one is doin' the same damn thing. I don' know what we're goin'ta do. Soren's goin' ta go crazy if we don' get things up'n runnin'!"

I press closer to the crowded sound booth, then clear my throat. A timid, squeaky voice emerges.

"Are you guys having some computer trouble?" I ask.

All heads turn in my direction, every man's face wearing a look of surprise when they see me.

"Yeah," the lead man says. "What's it to ya'?"

"I'm pretty good with computers," I say. "What do you have there, PC or Mac?"

"PC," the lead man says. "I doubt if you're gonna be able ta help. There's only five minutes ta show time."

"Do you mind if I have a look?" I ask.

"Might as well," he says. "Probably can't mess it up more'n it already is. Ralph, you wanna give Soren the bad news — tell 'im we might be delayed at least half an hour?"

"No," Ralph replies. "Why don't you tell him? He's going to be pissed. It's your job to keep the show running!"

"Just do it!" Ralph shouts, then he turns to me. "Okay, darlin', come over here and have a quick look."

I work my way through the crowd of sweaty male bodies until I'm in front of the large laptop computer and a cluster of display screens.

"So what's the problem, guys?" I ask, noticing that the display screens are blank, displaying only a blue pattern. A younger man, who seems to run the audio software, answers.

"The laptops boot up fine and my sound software runs good until I try to turn on the external screens. Then everything goes blank, including the laptop. I can't see the soundboard and can't control the sound."

"Can I try a couple of things?" I ask, looking to Ralph for approval.

"Go ahead," he says.

I reboot the laptop, then bring up the Command console. My fingers type out some commands from memory, allowing me to check for Interrupt conflicts. It isn't long before I find what I'm looking for — an IRQ conflict involving the video drivers. I exit the Command console and go to the Control Panel, looking for the installed video displays. I choose one and reset the IRQ setting for that display, then I reboot the laptop and double-click to start the sound-mixing software.

"Okay," I say to the younger man. "Try switching to the external monitors now." He takes control of the mouse, pulling down a menu and clicking on a command. Suddenly the external monitors come to life, showing a number of different displays.

"Well, I'll be damned," Ralph utters. "How'd *you* do that?" He turns to another man and shouts another command.

"Johnnie, run after Don and catch him before he gets to Soren. Tell 'im we're up and runnin' and we can start the show!"

"What's your name, sweetheart?" Ralph asks.

"Angela," I answer.

"Well, Angela, we're all truly thankful fer yer help. Soren'll be 'specially grateful. How'd ya know what t'do, anyhow?"

"I'm a bit of a computer geek," I answer. "Just happy I could help."

"Not as happy as me! I'll be sure to tell Soren how you helped us. Wher'ya sittin'?"

"My friend and I are in the front row, right of center," I reply.

"Well, you an' yer girlfriend enjoy the show."

"We will. If it's going to start in a couple of minutes, I guess I'd better get back to my seat. Goodbye," I say.

I feel a blush of pride as I almost run back down the center aisle. It's five minutes after seven and the crowd is growing restless, chanting for Pastor Soren.

"Where *were* you!" Dori admonishes, as I return to my seat. "The show almost started without you."

I grin at Dori. Just as I'm going to open my mouth to explain my absence, a well-dressed man walks onto the empty stage. The crowd jumps to its feet, screaming in anticipation of the start of Pastor Soren's ministry. The man raises a microphone and begins to speak.

"Hello, Cleveland!"

He waits while the crowd roars in unison, using his arms to urge the throng of admirers to make more noise.

"Are you ready to hear Pastor Soren's message of hope!"

The crowd goes wild again, starting to chant Soren's name in unison.

"Then I won't make you wait any longer. Ladies and gentlemen, I give you Pastor Soren Kristiansen!"

Dori and I jump up and down along with the crowd, screaming in excitement as an immaculately dressed man with curly blond hair takes the stage. I can't believe it. I'm only fifty feet from Pastor Soren Kristiansen!

I SENSE a feeling of loss creeping up on me. Pastor Soren's Ministry event is winding down, and I know it's going to be over soon. His choir is just finishing their final anthem, and the Pastor appears to be preparing for his final benediction.

"Friends, before I give the benediction, I want to take this opportunity to thank a very special person in the congregation tonight. This person was sent to us from God, like an angel, to ensure this event happened. Just before I was to come onstage tonight, my sound crew had a technical emergency that almost caused us to delay or cancel tonight's Ministry. But this special person appeared out of nowhere, and with her skill, she had our computer up and running in a matter of minutes. I would like to give my thanks personally… Angela… I heard that you're somewhere in the front row… where are you?… Give me a wave so I can see you."

I feel like I'm in a dream. Is he really talking to me? Suddenly I'm blinded by a brilliant beam of light. Instinctively my hand goes up to shield my eyes. The crowd is applauding and Dori is screaming in my ear.

"Angela. He's talking to you! Wave at him! Let him know it's you!" she screeches above the applause. I feel my face turning red with embarrassment. My arms move slowly until they're above my head, then I give the audience a timid-looking wave. The crowd rises to their feet, their applause growing steadily louder. Then Pastor Soren raises his arms dramatically, signaling to the crowd for silence. As if by magic, the crowd hushes instantly.

"Angela, I want to humbly thank you from the bottom of my heart, and I would like to do that in person. I would be most honored if you would come backstage after the conclusion of the Ministry, so that I can do just that. Just remain in your seat at the conclusion of the Ministry, and one of my assistants will come and bring you to me."

On cue, the spotlight leaves me. The only light remaining in the arena is focused on Pastor Soren. You can hear a pin drop as he pronounces the benediction to his enraptured flock.

I CAN'T STOP my legs from trembling as Pastor Soren's assistant leads us through a black curtain into the backstage area.

"The Pastor is greeting the local contest winners right now," she says. "If you'd be good enough to wait, he'd like to spend some time with you afterwards."

I look at Dori, whose eyes are as wide as I've ever seen them before.

"Angela, you didn't say anything… why didn't you tell me what you did?" she says, barely able to contain her excitement.

"I… I didn't get a chance. I just got back to my seat when the Ministry started. Besides, it isn't such a big deal. It only took me a couple of minutes to get the computer back online."

"Not a big deal!" she hisses. "You're getting a personal invitation to meet Pastor Soren, and it's not a big deal? This is the biggest thing that's ever happened to either one of us. You're a celebrity, girl!"

Pastor Soren looks up from his meet-and-greet and makes eye contact with me. The warmth of his smile almost makes me melt, and I struggle to keep my trembling legs from buckling. He signs one final autograph and shakes the lucky recipient's hand. Then he looks directly at us, and starts walking in our direction.

"Angela, my dear. Soren Kristiansen. I'm honored to meet you."

He extends his hand. Embarrassed, I raise a sweaty palm and my eyes lock onto his deep baby blues at the same moment. The sensation is like nothing I've ever experienced before. It isn't a sexual attraction. It feels like magnetism. It's like I'm being drawn under his spell and I'm helpless to resist.

"This… this… is my best friend, Dori. We're probably your two biggest fans."

How lame was that, Angela! You get your big chance to meet Pastor Soren and that's all you can come up with?

"Well, after what you did to help us out tonight, I would say that I'm probably one of *your* biggest fans," he chuckles. "So tell me about yourself, Angela. Where do you put your talents to use?"

"Umh… I have two kids, a ten-year-old daughter and an eight-year-old son." I feel myself blushing again. "We're living with my parents until my divorce goes through… until I can afford a place of my own."

"So what do you do for a living, my dear? And where did you get that delightful European accept? Every time you speak it sounds like you're singing."

I feel my ears getting hot and I know I'm blushing. I'm not used to being the center of attention, much less receiving flattering compliments from people I admire.

"I'm an accountant. I work in a small office for an old friend of my father's. My parents came from Hungary, so I suppose I got my accent from speaking Hungarian with them."

"And where did you learn so much about computers? Surely not working as an accountant."

"No. It's just my hobby. My boss doesn't even have a computer yet. I'm trying to convince him, but he still does everything the old fashioned way with a paper ledger."

"My goodness, dear lady. Somebody who is good with numbers *and* a genius with computers? You're wasting your talents. How would you like to come and work for me?"

I'm stunned. I can barely believe what I've just heard. My mind starts spinning, trying to figure out the implications of what he's offering.

Where would I live and work? Would I have to move the kids? Would David even allow that to happen? Can I afford to move?

"Angela, answer the man!" Dori urges. "Don't keep him waiting!"

"I'm sorry, Pastor. I'm a bit overwhelmed by your offer. Where would I be working, here in Cleveland?"

"Cleveland!" he snorts, then bursts out laughing. "Of course not. You'll be working in the Church's head office in New York City. The *World-Wide Community of Christ* is no longer just a small community church in Victoria, Canada. It's become a global force, with offices and missions across North America. And we're quickly spreading around the world!"

"New York?" I squeak. "I… I don't know. I've never even been outside Ohio. There's so much to think about."

"I understand completely," Pastor Soren says. He reaches into his suit pocket and produces a business card. "Take my card. Write down all of your questions, then phone me on Monday morning. I'll be in the New York office and I can answer your questions then."

"Thank you, Pastor. You have no idea how thankful I am right now."

"Not at all, my dear. As I said before, it is I who am thankful. Call me on Monday. It was a pleasure meeting you. You too, Dori. My assistant will make sure you find your way out of the building. Goodbye, until Monday!"

With that, Pastor Soren and his small entourage turn and start walking away. As they do, he turns his body and shouts back to me over his shoulder.

"And, Angela, if it's a question of money, you should know that I'm perfectly willing to pay whatever you ask, within reason."

With one last smile, he turns and disappears. Despite the endless questions swirling in my mind, I know already that I'm helpless to turn down the opportunity of a lifetime.

KNOWING I can't pass up the chance to work for Pastor Soren in New York, my biggest dilemma is moving my small family from our familiar little world in Cleveland, to a huge city like New York.

Where will we live? How can I afford to live there on one salary? How can I manage the kids without Momma and Papa's help?

"Why do you want to run off to the big city?" Papa says. "What's wrong with working for Walter Kovacs? He's a good man."

"Who is going to take care of the children?" Momma says. "In Cleveland we can help you. And when are they going to see their father? David still deserves to see them every weekend."

I feel bad when I think about taking Julia and Nicholas away from their dad. There's no doubt he'll make a big scene if I move them to New York. But I also know that David is all talk. Lately, he's been finding more excuses to miss his weekend visits. And I'm concerned that he might be drinking when he has them at his apartment. Somehow, I know he won't mind so much once we move. With David, the saying 'out of sight, out of mind' will most likely apply.

I'm sure that Julia and Nicholas will miss their *Nagyi* and *Papi* more than they'll miss their father. Momma and Papa have spent more time parenting the kids than I have, and they've certainly had a bigger influence on their lives than David.

Finally, I work out a compromise in my mind that I can live with. I blurt it out Sunday evening, after the kids are in bed and Momma and Papa are settled in front of the TV.

"Momma; Papa. I've decided to say yes to Pastor Soren," I say. "But I'm going to ask him if he'll let me do a six-month trial so I can figure out where we'll live, and whether I can afford to raise Julia and Nicholas in New York. They can finish their school year here in Cleveland, and start school in there in September. Of course, that depends totally on whether you're willing to take care of them until September. I promise that I'll fly home as often as I can during that time. And they can still have visits with David on weekends."

Papa looks out over his reading glasses at me and raises his eyebrows.

"You are sure about this?" he says. He looks at Momma for her answer. I see the worry on her face and tears forming in her eyes. She takes my hand in hers.

"Whatever you think is best, Angela," she says. "You know we love the children and we will do anything for them. We will miss them terribly after you move."

"I know, Momma," I say. "I doubt that I'll stay in New York forever. But it's just too good an opportunity for me to pass up. It will give me a chance to use the latest accounting software and my computer skills. As much as I appreciate Mr. Kovacs for hiring me, Papa, his way of doing things is more obsolete every year. And I know he's going to retire soon. I have to start looking out for my future!"

Papa nods. I see his reluctant acceptance of my logic on his face. I hug Momma, then I walk around the table and throw my arms around Papa's large frame.

"Thank you. I love you two so much, and I'll find a way to pay you both back. I promise. I'll call Pastor Soren tomorrow. If he still wants me, then I'll tell Julia and Nicholas after school."

That night, my mind and my heart are both racing as I lie in bed thinking about everything I'll need to do to ready myself for the move. New York City! I can hardly believe it. But that isn't the real source of my excitement. I'm going to be working side by side with Pastor Soren! Never in my wildest dreams did I think I would be this lucky. It almost feels too good to be true! It's only from sheer exhaustion that my mind finally switches itself off and succumbs to its need for sleep.

CHAPTER 3

MY FIRST month has flown by. I've found myself a tiny bachelor apartment on East 9th near the *World-Wide Community of Christ* offices. I can walk to work, taking in the sights, sounds, smells, and tastes of New York culture. To my amazement, by the end of that first month, I'm no longer feeling like a fish out of water.

I've spent my first month learning the ins and outs of the WWCC accounting system, finding out that the church's financial structure is a good deal more complicated than I'd ever imagined. In addition to the church's online and touring Ministries and Missions, I'm amazed to find out that it is investing heavily in real estate across the country. So far I haven't got into the details of the church's financial workings, but I realize I still have plenty to learn.

Julia and Nicholas are both excited and reticent about the possibility of moving to New York during the summer. I'm glad that they feel safe and secure living in Momma and Papa's home. And as much as I worry about David and his drinking, it's important for my children to still know they have one parent nearby.

It's Monday morning, the first day back after my first weekend visit to Cleveland. I've only been at my desk for a couple of minutes, waiting for my computer to boot, when my phone rings.

"Angela, Soren here," says the familiar voice. "Are you busy today? Would you be able to meet with me about a special project that's come up?"

"Of course," I answer. "Can I ask what it's about?"

"Do you know anything about computer viruses?" Soren asks. "My IT team has been noticing some attempts to hack into our servers over the past two weeks, and I'm going to need some more people working on security. I told them about your skills and told them I wanted you to join them for a while. I hope you don't mind."

"Not at all, sir," I say, trying to hide the excitement in my voice at being able to increase my computer skills. "But what about my accounting responsibilities? I've just got up to speed on the system and I'm supposed to be increasing my workload."

"Don't you worry about that," Soren replies. "And stop calling me *sir*, for Pete's sake. Please call me Soren. You're part of the Ministry now."

"Yes, s…" I begin, catching myself just in time. "Of course,… Soren. When would you like to meet?"

"How about meeting me for lunch, then I'll introduce you to the IT team right afterwards. That will give me a chance to find out how you've been getting along here in the office, and in New York. I'll meet you in reception at eleven-thirty."

"Thank you. I'll be ready and waiting," I answer.

I realize my legs are trembling as I hang up the phone. I know Pastor Soren is an incredibly busy man. He only spends a few days in the New York office each month, having to split his time between the WWCC home church and his family in Victoria, being on the road with his Ministry, and managing the church's business in New York. I haven't spent more than twenty minutes in his presence in my first month in the office, so I feel excited about being asked to join his special project, and to be able to discuss his plans over lunch.

Angela, why didn't you wear something dressier today? You're not dressed for going out to lunch!

I need to make some last-minute touch-ups to my makeup, so I reach for my purse and hurry to the Ladies' room. As I look into the mirror, I'm embarrassed by what I see. I'm wearing the same conservative white blouse and dark skirt I've been wearing almost every day since I started working for Mr. Kovacs in Cleveland. At almost forty years old, I try to ignore the crow's feet forming at the corner of my eyes. I reach for my makeup and do my best to cover the wrinkles and put more color into my cheeks.

I shake my head sadly as I look at my fading blonde hair. It's the same shoulder-length style I've been wearing for almost ten years. So far, my first grey hairs are blending into the naturally curly blonde background and are barely noticeable. But I see how they dull the normal bright sheen I used to see in the mirror. I find myself making a resolution.

It's time for a new style… maybe even some color. You're living in New York now. Time to try on a more modern look. You're going to book yourself a makeover tomorrow!

I finish making touch-ups to my face and assess my handiwork in the mirror. I start feeling a sense of excitement in my body as I imagine spending one-on-one time with Pastor Soren. I walk back to my cubicle and my desk, but I can't focus on work. My mind won't stop thinking of my impending lunch date. I keep looking at the clock — eleven-thirty can't come soon enough.

"HAVING SUCH a popular website is both a blessing and a curse," Soren observes. "We're blessed to have so many people watching our online

Ministry, meeting other believers in our chat rooms, and making donations to our Missions. But most of our believers don't know the first thing about keeping their computers secure. Would you agree?"

"Oh, definitely," I reply. "Most of them don't install their Windows updates or their anti-virus definitions. Actually, most of them probably don't even have anti-virus software running on their machines."

"Exactly," Soren adds. "Or they blindly open every email that lands in their *Inbox* and open up attachments without thinking. They have no idea that they might have just activated a virus that could be reading their passwords for every website they access, including their banks!"

"I agree," I say, feeling good that Soren and I are on the same page when it comes to internet security. "Most people think I'm stupid to be so worried about the security on my computer. But, since you're talking to me about it right now, I'm guessing that it's starting to affect our network."

"Yes. We've detected a few attempts over the last month to penetrate our network. Ordinarily, we wouldn't be concerned, but the attacks seem to be increasing in sophistication, and we don't have anybody in the department who is up to date on the latest tactics that hackers are using. That's why I asked you here. From what you showed me in Cleveland, you're an excellent self-learner. I'd like you to find out what you can from the rest of the team about the recent attacks on our system, and I'd like you to learn about the current state of hacking, so we can fortify our defenses. Just let me know what resources you need, and I'll get them for you. Your budget is open-ended, within reason. We save a lot of financial information about our customers on our server, and it would be a catastrophe if somebody hacked into our system and stole it."

I gulp and I feel my ears getting hot. I'm embarrassed at how much confidence Soren is showing in me.

"Are you sure?" I ask. "It's not really an area I know much about. I have a lot of learning to do."

"Of course I'm sure," he says. "I know that you're capable of learning. And by the way, there's just one more thing. You'll report directly to me on this project until we have something to share with the rest of the IT group."

Now I'm confused. I feel my forehead wrinkle and my eyes betraying my lack of understanding.

"You don't understand?" Soren asks. "Actually, it's quite simple. The rest of the team is so busy with our day to day activities, that I need additional help. That's one of the reasons I hired you. Once you get up to speed, I'm going to put you in charge of network security."

I can't believe what I've just heard. I feel my entire face heating up with embarrassment this time.

"I'm so flattered, Soren," I say. "I hope I can live up to your confidence in me."

"I'm sure you will," he says, trying to reassure me. He reaches out and puts his hand over top of mine. My mind starts racing, wondering what is happening. It's been a long time since a man has touched my hand that way. I feel confused. But he simply pats my hand twice, then removes it after holding it for a few seconds.

"I have all the confidence in the world in you, my dear," he adds. "I've seen what you can do, Angela. You have a God-given talent for understanding computers. I just want to give you the chance to live up to your full potential. As soon as possible, I want you to learn everything there is to learn about our network."

"Well, thank you," I mumble. I'm starting to believe that Soren's touch was nothing more than showing his reassurance and confidence in me. I manage to make eye contact with him again.

"Now, enough about business," he says, abruptly changing the subject. "Let's enjoy the rest of our lunch hour. Tell me more about yourself."

"There's not a lot to tell," I answer. "What would you like to know?"

"When we met, you told me that you have two children and you are going through a divorce. That must be very difficult. Why don't you tell me all about it?"

Before I know it, I'm spilling my entire life story to Pastor Soren, glad to have somebody in New York who is willing to listen.

Then, before I realize it, I see Soren looking at his watch.

"Oh my God, I've been talking nonstop. What time is it?" I ask. We're supposed to be back in the office at twelve thirty to meet with the IT team.

"It's one o'clock," he says. "But don't worry, I've been so engrossed in your story, I didn't even notice. I'll make a quick call to the office to tell them I'm running a bit late. Believe me, it happens more often than you can imagine."

I find myself blushing, embarrassed that I've revealed so much about myself. Soren smiles at me, as he notices my red face.

"Don't worry, my dear. I enjoyed getting to know you."

"Thank you," I gushed. "You seem to have a way of putting people at ease."

"I wouldn't be much of a pastor if didn't listen to my flock, would I?" he says. We both laugh.

I can't believe how Soren has managed to put me at ease so quickly. By the time we leave the restaurant, I feel like we've known each other for much longer than one month.

"I CAN'T BELIEVE how much I've learned about computer security and hacking over the past three weeks," I say to Dori.

I see her eyes glazing over. It's the one thing that separates us. While I'm a computer nerd, Dori barely knows how to send an email. I had to write down the instructions for her so she could remember how to sign into the WWCC chat rooms. But in every other aspect, a stranger would think we were sisters, we're so much alike.

"Angela! You're living in New York City, the most exciting city in the world. And you're working for Pastor Soren, the hottest pastor on the planet. Aren't you doing *anything* exciting after work?"

"Don't you mean, *am I out hunting for a new man?*" I answer.

"Of course I do," Dori squeals. "What else do you think I mean!"

"Well, I'm not a social butterfly, and you know that. So I have to do *something* with my spare time in New York. I might as well learn as much as I can about hacking, so I don't have to think about it when I'm here in Cleveland with Julia and Nicholas."

"So, what's it like working with *him*?" Dori asks, changing back to her favorite subject.

"You've got a one-track mind, don't you," I say, shaking my head and laughing at the same time. "Well, for one thing, I'm finding out that the church is much bigger than I ever thought. The computer system and the financial structure are a lot like a major company. There's so much more to learn."

"Not the *church*, silly. *Him!* What's it like working with Pastor Soren? Is he really that hot in person?"

"Dori, he's married. He's got a wife and little boy! He's got their pictures front and center on his desk."

But he touched you on the hand!

Seeing the blush on my face, Dori continues her inquisition, undeterred.

"Well…?" she asks.

No he didn't. That was an accident. Don't be crazy. He's a pastor, he wouldn't be hitting on you!

"He's only in the office for a couple of days, every fourth week, Dori. I only meet with the man once a month. There's nothing going on with Pastor Soren, okay? Get your mind out of the gutter."

"Then why were you blushing?" she accuses.

Yeah, why are you blushing like a school girl, Angela?

"Because you're embarrassing me, Dori. How can you even think that I'd be involved with Soren?"

"Oh, so it's *Soren* now," she taunts. "What happened to *Pastor Soren*?"

"You are such a naughty girl. Come on, get your mind out of the gutter. Can't we talk about something else?" I ask.

"Okay," Dori says, pouting. "So what's the shopping like? Have you got lots of new clothes? Show me everything you've bought."

I gaze at Dori's excited face. I envy her. She's so spontaneous and exuberant. Yet, at other times, she seems like she's a much younger, more immature little sister. But I don't let it bother me. It's who she is, and I still love her like she's the younger sister I never had. I put my arms around Dori and embrace her.

"I've missed you, Dori," I say. I feel her tightening her grip on me.

"I've missed you too, Angela," she whispers. I think I hear Dori sniffling, and I feel tears welling up in my eyes. My arms release their grip on her.

"Okay, let me show you what I've bought so far. But I warn you, it isn't much."

We take each other by the hand and I pull Dori towards the closet in my old bedroom at Momma and Papa's house. I throw open the closet door and Dori's eyes grow wide with excitement. She starts pulling hangers of my clothes off the rack, just like old times. For a moment, it almost feels I never left home at all — like New York is a million miles away.

IT'S DIFFICULT to believe that a month has passed since my last meeting with Soren. I'm sitting beside him in a secluded circular booth in the back of a nearby Italian restaurant. I'm nervous, trying to find a way to ask him about the questions I've raised while scrutinizing the WWCC network and its finances.

"Soren, I think I'm pretty much up to speed on our network and I'm starting to understand where our security vulnerabilities might be. So the IT part of me is feeling good about the project. But the accountant side of me is confused."

"Oh? What on earth is troubling you, my dear?" he says.

I feel a lump forming in my throat. My heart is pounding. It feels like it's taking an eternity to answer.

Answer him, Angela. He's going to wonder what's wrong with you!

I clear my throat, and suddenly my words seem to start flowing on their own volition.

"Well, I'm pretty clear on how all of our different church activities interface with the network. I see where broadcasting the services fits, and where we collect the donations for the church and its Ministries. And I can see where the money from the real estate arm of the church goes, but I can't tell where the income originates. It seems to be coming from an external source — one or more extremely large sources."

I think I see the smile disappear from Soren's face for a heartbeat, but I can't be sure. When I look back into his eyes a second later, all I see is the same warm, reassuring smile that I've learned to recognize as his trademark.

"Ahhh, you're referring to the South American income," he says, nodding to confirm what I had found. "Of course. How could I have been so absentminded to not tell you about that? The South American countries are a hotbed of Christianity, and our biggest area of growth. But we needed to have both Spanish and Portuguese versions of our website. So we contracted with another company to build South American websites to mirror our English site. They are much more lucrative than our North American site. We funnel all of the net South American income directly into the real estate arm of the church for investment."

"That's a bit unorthodox, isn't it? Wouldn't we be reporting it as income from foreign sources?"

"Yes, for most countries that would be the case. But things are much more complicated in South America, so all of that money is accounted for in the South American countries. We've received a great deal of legal guidance on this issue, and the funds going into the real estate arm of our church have already been reported and accounted for in

South America. We're simply transferring the funds from one arm of our church to another. Quite legitimately, I might add."

Not being knowledgeable at all about international tax law, I decide to drop the issue.

"Okay, I'll leave that up to the international tax lawyers. That's way out of my league," I admit, laughing nervously.

Soren laughs heartily as he wipes his mouth with a serviette.

"That's what I say. I don't understand it either. That's why we pay the international tax lawyers such good money — so we can relax and focus on our Ministry."

"So, now that I'm up to speed and understand our network, what do you want me to do next?" I ask.

"I want you to become a cyber thief," he answers.

I stare at him in disbelief, lost for words. In the deafening silence between us, I hear the sounds of laughter, clinking glasses, and cutlery clinking on plates, coming from all around me.

Soren suddenly ends the awkward silence by breaking into hearty laughter.

"I got you there," he says, laughing at the blank look on my face. He continues to roar with laughter at my look of disbelief. Gradually he manages to calm himself, then he assumes a more serious look.

"Seriously, Angela. I want you to play with our network as if you were a cyber thief. I want you to find every conceivable way that somebody could hack into our network to steal money from our members, and from the church. I want you to become a hacker. By doing so, I want you to design a security system that will thwart any attempt to hack into it. The best way to stop a thief is to think like a thief, wouldn't you say?"

I nodded my head slowly in agreement. On the surface, I couldn't argue with his logic.

"When do I start?" I ask hesitantly.

"The sooner the better," Soren replies. "Not only do I want you to do this in theory, I want you to actually show me what you find. I want to see what it would look like on our network. Once you've done that, then we'll start working on what we have to do to plug all the holes, so we're certain we don't have any security leaks."

"I guess I can do that," I answer. "I'll plan on reporting to you when you're back in New York next month. Will that do?"

"It most certainly will," he answers.

"One more thing," I add. "I'll need a laptop. The newest, fastest one I can get, so I can work from my apartment or when I'm back in Cleveland. I'm going to need a lot of processing power for hacking. Can you make that happen?"

"Of course. Go out and order what you need and give me the invoices. I'll take care of everything. So how are those two fine children of yours doing back in Cleveland?" he says, changing the subject suddenly.

His question catches me off guard. At first, I don't notice him sliding around the circular seat so that he's closer to me, then he places his hand gently on my back. I feel my body freeze, as it did the first time I felt his hand touching mine. Once again, I feel a flood of confusing thoughts surge through my brain. I try to control my breathing, without showing my anxiety. I'm at a loss, unable to make sense of the situation. Then once again, as quickly as it occurred, his hand is gone, and he resumes talking as if nothing happened.

"Are they adjusting well to your being in New York?" he asks. His voice is gentle and his smile is warm and inviting.

But it's too late. I've already gone into automatic mode. Part of me starts talking about myself and my family, as if we were old friends. That part is flattered at the attention from Soren. But at the same time, other very young parts of me are on full alert — the parts that remember being abused many years ago by Michael Farkas. They are screaming a warning to the rest of my being.

This is no accident! Get away from him! This is wrong!

I feel as if it was Michael who just placed his hand on my back, not Soren. The adult inside me keeps trying to tell me that Soren's touch was that of a gentle, compassionate pastor. But, unlike our previous meeting, that part of me is now having more difficulty believing what it is saying. Instead, it hears the young voices from my past shouting their warning from within. I force myself to come back into the present. I slowly become aware of the artificial smile I'm wearing on my face. The young, terrified parts of me that remember Michael's abuses, are slowly retreating into dark corners of my memory. I am gradually coming back into the moment and feeling the warmth of Soren's pastoral voice.

I start to feel more like a whole person again. My smile gradually becomes more genuine. I slowly open up, telling Soren more and more about my family and my personal life. He has a way of doing that with people. Against my better judgment, he is once again making me feel like I can open up and trust him with anything. I don't know it yet, but I have a lot to learn.

I'VE THROWN myself into my new project over the past three weeks, ordering the fastest laptop I could find online. I've been reading voraciously, teaching myself the differences between a Trojan, a worm and a virus. I've learned how to use ports in the Windows operating system as back doors for worms to insert themselves on victim computers. And I've learned how easy it is to trick people into clicking their mouse on phoney web pages, or to open attachments in phoney emails, allowing Trojans to burrow their way into a victim's operating system. I've learned about Botnets and how worms and Trojans can turn a victim's computer into a foot soldier in a giant army of computers, controlled by unseen cybercriminals.

The most frightening piece of information I found is how many people never update their Windows software to close their computer's back doors. And how many of them never use or update anti-virus software, and never use more than one password for everything they do on their computers. They are the easy targets.

But my interests are in finding ways to beat other savvy hackers. I need to find out how they gain access into servers where the real rewards are stored — databases full of usernames and passwords, credit card numbers and personal information that can be used for identity theft.

Strangely enough, my ultimate target is the *World-Wide Community of Christ* and its network server. It's now my job to see how secure our network is. From what I've read online, there are hacking kits that are readily available for purchase on the internet, so that even a novice hacker like myself can create sophisticated cyber-attacks on servers like ours at the WWCC.

I have two main goals to accomplish before I meet with Soren in two weeks: to show him how easy it is for somebody to hack into the WWCC network, and to show how easy it is for somebody to exploit the computers of our church members.

It's a lazy Saturday evening, and I've just finished talking to Julia, Nicholas, and my parents in Cleveland. It's only been a week since I've seen them, but already I'm feeling lonely. I decide to make a cup of coffee, and then search the internet for a hacking kit to suit my purposes.

Still not believing that hacker kits are so readily available on the internet, I take a shot in the dark. I do a simple Google search for *hacker kits*, and I can barely believe the massive search result that appears on my screen. Who knew that the market was so large for selling kits to teach people how to hack? And all I had to do was Google it!

I click on the first site in my search. I laugh as I read the site's rationale for their product: *For ethical hackers and network administrators who want to identify vulnerable network access points.*

Right. Ethical hackers. As if such a thing exists. I suppose it will only be 'ethical hackers' who try to break into big computer networks like Uncle Sam's. They'll probably try to claim that any U.S. citizen should have the right to access secure information anytime they like. Right! And I'm sure it's only going to be legitimate network administrators like me who want to use these kits.

I pay the seventy-nine dollar fee, wondering just how safe my credit card information is with this 'ethical' vendor, then I download the software.

I'm blown away! After spending only about fifteen minutes learning the software, I start doing a scan of the WWCC website. Within twenty seconds, the scan returns a detailed report with a long list of vulnerabilities — it includes not only the few I've already identified on my own, but many more. The list is extensive and frightening. It reads like a guided roadmap into our network. Also embedded in the hacking software are tools for compiling code to penetrate those vulnerabilities. Within an hour, I have created a worm that works its way through the back door and inside our network. All I had to do was create a simple buffer overflow at one of our vulnerable Windows ports. No username or password needed. It accesses the list of all network users, including WWCC church members, along with their usernames, passwords, and email addresses. Just like that!

It gets me thinking.

Okay. If I'm one of the bad guys, what would I do with this information? What's the worst thing I could do?

It doesn't take me long to realize that the ultimate prize for a hacker would be getting the banking information from unsuspecting victims. My plan starts to gel. I need to plant a Trojan on the computers of WWCC members who log into our network, using the WWCC network as my own personal robot.

Now that my hacker's toolkit has written some code to create a worm to infiltrate the WWCC network, I need to write some more elaborate code for a Trojan that will hide within the network and avoid detection. The goal is for the Trojan to become activated whenever a church member logs onto our network. When that happens, it will activate another worm that infiltrates the member's computer, just as I've hacked into the WWCC network. In a real life attack, it would be the worm's task to plant a Trojan virus that would read the user's username and password for their credit card or PayPal accounts when they're making donations to the church.

I'll collect a list of users, their passwords, and payment information to prove to Soren how easily it can be done.

So I set to work. By midnight, I'm finished. My worm is now buried in the WWCC network, waiting for church members to log into the church network. All I have to do now is wait for it to send the Trojan out to infect the church members' computers, to collect their payment information, then to send it back to my laptop. I should have all the information I need to present to Soren within a few days.

Mission accomplished. I'm now officially a hacker! The reality starts to sink in and it's quite terrifying. Anybody who knows how to write code and has a malevolent heart can buy a toolkit online that will give them the tools to roam the internet, looking for computers and networks to explore and exploit. And I could be one of those malevolent persons if I choose.

CHAPTER 4

MY LAPTOP is set up on the meeting table in Soren's office. I've just finished presenting the final slide of my PowerPoint presentation. The lights are dim. I'm proud of what I've accomplished for Pastor Soren, since I desperately want to make a professional impression. I'm dressed in the new suit I bought for the occasion, and I've cut my hair short. I even unbuttoned the expensive new white blouse one more button than I've ever dared before. I was pleased with what I saw in the mirror before I left for work. I look confident, and dare I say, even sexy.

"Very impressive presentation, my dear," Soren says. "You've been a busy girl."

"Thank you, sir," I reply. "But you really have to see it in action on a computer to appreciate it."

"What's with the *sir?*" he says. "We're all family here. My name is Soren — I insist."

"Of course… Soren," I stammer. I'm still uncomfortable calling this important man by his first name.

"Just watch closely, and you'll see my presentation in action," I said.

I close the PowerPoint presentation, leaving my computer's desktop as the background on the projection screen. A black window on the desktop flashes the white Command Prompt, waiting for me to type a command. My fingers click away for a few seconds, then I hit the <Enter> key. The window goes black momentarily, then a larger window opens. In that window, my computer is logged into a user account on the WWCC network. Soren's name flashes at the top of the window. I've just hacked into his user account.

"I hope you don't mind, sir… I mean, Soren. I didn't think my presentation would have had as much impact if I didn't do this."

I look at Soren's face. It is devoid of expression as he processes the implications of what I've just done.

I've gone too far… I just screwed up. Now I'm in big trouble.

Suddenly Soren's face illuminates. His head tips back and he roars with laughter. He keeps nodding in approval as he howls. When he finally calms down, he puts his hand on my shoulder.

"Well played, my dear. You have definitely got my full attention. What's next?" His hand remains on my shoulder. I'm not sure whether I feel uncomfortable or proud.

"We have to buy some sophisticated anti-virus software for our server," I continue. "It only took me half an hour to break into our network. And any high school kid who knows how to write code and download a kit off the internet can do it too. Once they're into our network, they can use it to do anything they want, like stealing money from you and me, or from our church members. Our software has to continuously scan the Windows ports for vulnerabilities. Then it needs to close them to prevent access through buffer overloads."

As I'm talking, I feel Soren's hand slide down from my shoulder until it rests on my hip. As it does, I find myself staring at a framed portrait on his desk. Ironically, it is a portrait of Soren, his wife, and his son. I can't take my eyes off his wife. He starts talking before I can open my mouth to protest.

"You've done excellent work, Angela. Once again, you've surprised me with your resourcefulness. I like the way you think. You're a lot like me. You're not afraid to think outside the box. I think we can do great things together."

The situation is starting to feel very creepy. His hand remains resting firmly on my hip. My heart is pounding and I feel myself starting to perspire.

Soren moves closer to me, and at the same time I feel his arm starting to curl around my waist, then slide down over the curves of my butt. Suddenly, my chest is rigid and I'm having difficulty breathing. I move my lips to say *Stop*, but nothing comes out. My mind flies back into childhood. I feel like I'm eleven years old again. I feel Michael Farkas's fingers moving over my private parts. My body is frozen in fear, and I feel helpless to stop the unwanted assault. I feel dirty and ashamed.

Before I know it, Soren has pulled my body against his, and his lips are coming towards mine. Instinctively, I push him away with both arms, breaking free of his embrace. I finally find my voice.

"Pastor… Soren… What are you doing? You're married! I can't do this!" My mind is racing, trying to think of ways to talk myself out of the real-life nightmare that is unfolding. "You're a man of God. We'd be breaking His Commandment," I implore.

"Now, now, Angela. Don't overreact. You know I've felt a bond growing between us, ever since that night we met. It was fate. Don't you think that God meant to bring us together that night? If the Biblical scholars are right, then even our Lord Jesus sought comfort with Mary Magdalene every once in a while. How can we deny ourselves the pleasures of the flesh when God Himself has brought us together?"

"I can't… it's… it's just not right. Please don't do this," I whimper.

Now I'm begging. I feel trapped. If I say yes, I'm betraying myself. I feel no physical attraction for Soren. My admiration for him has just vanished like the wind. But he's my boss and my sole source of income for raising my children. If I continue to say no, I know my days with the WWCC and in New York are numbered. I look at his face. His forehead is creased, and the sparkle has disappeared from his eyes. I see that it's been replaced by a look of desperation, and possibly the beginnings of anger.

"Angela," he begs. "Give yourself some time to think about it. I'm flying to Florida for some Ministries this week. Come with me. You've earned a vacation. We can talk things over. God means for us to be together. You'll see!"

Find a way to put him off for a while, Angela. Don't commit yourself now. Find a way to buy yourself some time!

"I… I'll think about it," I blurt. "You might be right. Maybe it is fate. But I need some time to think. This is so sudden. Can you do that for me, Soren?"

Soren's face softens. The lines of concern that were etched in his forehead, now vanish. His face comes alive again and the sparkle returns to his eyes.

"That's my girl. Of course I can give you some time."

"You'll be back in New York in three weeks, right?" I said. "We have to meet again so I can report on my progress with patching our security holes. Why don't we go out to dinner when you get back? Let's see if we still feel the same way then," I suggest.

"That's a marvelous suggestion, my dear. I'll take you out for a night in New York that you'll never forget," he says, winking.

"I'll look forward to that," I lie. I can't look him in the eye. I don't know what else to say. An awkward silence begins to fill the room.

Before it becomes any more uncomfortable, the calm is shattered by the electronic beeping of Soren's phone. He steps away from me and reaches for the phone. As he does, and as I try to slow down my breathing, I can't stop staring at the family portrait on his desk, thinking about what I would be doing to his wife and son.

"Umh hmm," Soren mumbles. "Yes… uh huh… that's fine… that's great news. Tell them I can drop in on my way home from Florida next week. Okay… great… yes, I'm just finishing up here. Why don't you come down to my office and you can fill me in on the details? Okay, I'll see you in five minutes," he says, then sets the receiver in its cradle.

"Ah, yes. Where were we? Dinner. Just you and me for a night on the town, next time I'm back in New York. Agreed?" he says. His eyes are half pleading, but also demanding, as they connect with mine.

"Agreed," I say. I allow him to place his hands on my shoulders again, while he leans towards me and gives me a kiss on one cheek.

"I'll have a complete report on the security situation when you get back," I repeat.

That gives me just three weeks to figure out how I'm going to get out of this mess. I don't know how I'll do it, but I have to find a way!

MY WORLD has turned upside-down since the assault by Soren. I'm still feeling dirty and riddled with guilt, and I'm now completely disillusioned with the man I had previously idolized. My Catholic upbringing has trained me well. I'm supposed to respect and trust men of the cloth. And yet, this man of God attacked me against my wishes. I'm now questioning everything I had previously thought about Soren Kristiansen. Even though part of me knows he was wrong, another part of my mind still refuses to accept that he isn't the saint that I'd created in my mind. That part of me is starting to realize how I've idolized him out of my desperate need to belong and to believe in something important.

It's taken days for my brain to stop ruminating about my predicament, and to be able to start focusing on my work again. I'm still having trouble focusing on fixes for our network security. It just doesn't seem important anymore.

And I'm second-guessing my little demonstration of how powerful and destructive a Trojan can be. It was the kind of information I didn't want to see in the hands of somebody with questionable ethics. And right now, I'm definitely having second thoughts about Soren's morals and ethics.

As much as I've learned about computers and hacking in the past few weeks, I'm still an accountant by trade. Something else has been nagging at me for days, but I haven't been able to figure out what it is. I log into my Bank of America online account, checking my balance to see if I can afford a second flight back to Cleveland this month. I'm missing Julia, Nicholas, Momma, Papa, and Dori more than ever after my recent incident with Soren. As I gaze at the list of debits and deposits to my account, I suddenly realize what has been nagging at me.

Bank accounts! The unexplained flood of income into the church's real estate account! I realize that Soren's explanation for that income hasn't been sitting right with me.

I log out of Bank of America. I bring up the WWCC web page, ready to log into the WWCC network with my own username and password, then I stop myself. I don't have security clearance to look into the part of the network I really want to see, like the real estate account. I can't see where the income is coming from. But I need to know. There is much more to Soren Kristiansen than he shows on the surface, and I'm determined to find out what he's hiding.

I start typing in the *Login* window. But instead of using my username and password, I use Soren's information in the *User* and *Password* boxes — information I collected with my demonstration virus. Magically, Pandora's Box opens up in front of me. I now have complete access to the network and I can explore as I please. I open the Network control panel in Windows, noting two network connections that I can't explain. I write down the IP addresses of the two unexplained connections.

I open the hacker's toolkit on my laptop. I start by trying to identify the IP addresses, but the toolkit can't attach an identity. Then I explore for vulnerable ports in those systems. The report for the first server comes up blank. Wherever this server is, it is extremely secure. Now I'm puzzled. If the other server is so secure, how is our system connecting with it? I realize I need to find which program on our server is connecting with the unidentified network. My search is in vain. I can't find any information on the network that will allow me to connect to the mystery networks. I've reached a roadblock.

What are those two networks, and how is Soren connecting to them?

I get up from my desk and go to my apartment window. Sipping my coffee, I gaze out the window at the Manhattan skyline in the distance, and the Saturday hustle and bustle on the street below. The novelty of New York is wearing off. I'm homesick for my children and my parents. I miss Cleveland and Dori. I sit down on the built-in bench that lines the inside of my apartment's bay window. A lone tear begins its solitary journey down my cheek. My thoughts wander aimlessly and I gaze back towards my desk at my laptop.

All of a sudden, something clicks in my mind.

The laptop! Of course... Soren's laptop... If he's hiding something, he isn't going to access it from the WWCC network. He's only there one week each month. He's using his own laptop!

Now I have a new mission. I need to plant my own Trojan on Soren's laptop.

AS IT turns out, getting the Trojan into Soren's laptop via an email was a piece of cake. He had no reason to suspect an email from someone in the WWCC inner circle. The small piece of executable code that I'd planted on his laptop computer has almost finished its job. An external hard drive, attached to my own laptop, is clicking and humming away, creating a mirror image of his laptop's hard drive. Every time he connects to the internet from now on, the duplicate image on my external drive will synchronize with his laptop. The small black window on my screen flashes a simple message after the Command Prompt. *Disk image created.*

I feel my heart pounding, knowing that what I'm about to do goes against every moral value I've ever held. I am now a cyber thief, trespassing on somebody else's property. I'm entering into the murky world of Soren Kristiansen. On one hand, I'm afraid of what I might discover. On the other, I understand that I have to know if there's a dark side to the man I used to idolize.

I reboot my laptop, this time starting it from the external hard drive — the clone of Soren's laptop. In a matter of a couple of minutes, I've left my own world behind, and I'm seeing the world through the eyes of Pastor Soren Kristiansen's personal laptop.

I LOOK at the time on my computer. It's two-thirty a.m. — six hours since I'd rebooted my computer. I still can't stop exploring.

My hands tremble as I click my mouse and delve more deeply into Soren's world. What I've found so far is beyond belief. The face of the man I had admired is merely a mask. The more I explore, the more I realize that Soren Kristiansen only wanted people to see what he wanted them to see. In reality, he is hardly a man of God. Even more disconcerting is the reality that he has very powerful friends in high places. How Soren Kristiansen has managed to get an account somewhere within the U.S. Government is hard to believe.

Who does he know, and in what kinds of spying is he involved?

Amongst my most shocking discoveries are the businesses that the good Pastor is running on the side. He is the mastermind behind internet scams based in Nigeria and Asia. I think about how many obviously fraudulent spam emails I receive in a week, then I realize that Soren's enterprises are responsible for many of them.

But even worse are the online pornography sites I've discovered. I've managed to trace them back to IP addresses in Vietnam that belong to travel agencies. He appears to be hiding those enterprises behind a legitimate business façade — the developing tourist industry in that country. He has bank accounts in Hong Kong and Switzerland, into which the income from his illicit business activities are diverted. I have no doubt that those bank accounts are the source of the money that flows like a river into the WWCC real estate enterprise. The accountant in me realizes that I've finally found the answer to the question that has been plaguing me for weeks.

He's using the WWCC to launder money!

I nod to myself, part of me appreciating the complexity of Soren's financial web.

But then I click on more email messages, each one becoming more eye-opening and disturbing than the last. In those messages, he brags that he has branched into the world of identity theft. He is exchanging ideas with business associates about building a giant Botnet — a worldwide network of infected computers that could collect personal information and banking information from unsuspecting computer owners around the world. I find my body shaking with disbelief as I read email after email that exposes the extent of his criminal activities.

Good Lord, look at this! He's even buying fake passports and driver's licenses — just in case he has to leave his Pastor Soren identity behind!

Then I open the email that will change my life. Soren is boasting to somebody, whom he addresses only by a code name: *Helen*. He has found somebody who is a gifted computer wizard, who can help them develop the Botnet. All he has to do is draw her into his illegal activities until she is over her head. After that, she won't dare try to walk away.

'... she won't dare try to walk away...'

The realization hits me with the impact of a runaway train. *My God... he's talking about me! What have I got myself into? ... And how am I going to get myself out?*

CHAPTER 5

MY MIND is still scrambling for ideas as I ride the elevator to the top floor and the WWCC offices. I know I can't stall Soren much longer. I have to find a way to discourage him from creating his Botnet. More importantly, I have to find a way to end his creepy physical advances and let him down gently. Neither task is going to be easy. Once again, I'm wearing my new suit and blouse, but this time I've done up an extra button to discourage any view of my cleavage.

"Good morning, Angela." The cheery voice of our receptionist, Jeanette, interrupts my ruminations. "Pastor Soren is waiting for you in his office."

Just great! I wasn't counting on meeting with him so soon. I need to go over my game plan once more.

"Thanks, Jeanette," I say, pasting a smile over my worried face. "I just have to dump some stuff in my office. Tell him I'll be over in a couple of minutes."

I unlock the door to my office, and then set my computer bag down on the desk, quickly unzipping a compartment to remove the laptop and my report. I take a deep breath and rehearse my plan once more in my head.

Don't give him time to talk about security or the report. Give him your notice right away. Remember, it's because you're homesick for Cleveland — not just the kids. Then give him the report and your recommendations for the IT department. They can do the follow-up. Make it quick and make it clean. You can do it.

After one last deep breath, I swing the door open, throw my shoulders back, walk confidently down the hallway to Soren's office, and knock on the door.

"Come in," he calls.

I stride into his office, exuding confidence in myself and in my plan.

"Have a seat, my dear," Soren says, motioning to the conversation area in the corner of the office. "It's wonderful to see you again. Time flies. I can't believe that you've been working for us for four months already. Are you enjoying New York and working here with us?"

Okay, Angela. Here's your big chance. He's set you up for the perfect segue.

"I can't thank you enough for the experience," I begin. "But before we begin discussing my report, I'm afraid there's something I have to discuss with you."

"Oh," Soren says, raising his eyebrows in surprise. "What is it?"

"Well,…," I begin. "You know I agreed to try the job, and to try living in New York for six months so I could see whether it would work for me and the kids."

"Yes, of course," Soren answers. "Go on."

"Umh…," I stammer. I feel my self-confidence abandoning me and my knees start trembling. "I realize that I'm terribly homesick for Cleveland, not just Julia and Nicholas. It's everything — the city, my friends, my parents — I miss it all terribly. I'm so grateful for the opportunity you've given me, and for everything I've learned. But I just don't think New York is right for me or my children. So, I'm giving you my notice that I'll finish out my last two months, and I'll finish off the security project before I leave."

There! You did it, girl! Good job!

I feel my knees stop trembling, and a weight seems to be lifting from my shoulders.

"I'm terribly disappointed to hear that," Soren replies. "I really am. I had such big plans for you. I don't suppose there's anything I can say that will change your mind?"

"I'm afraid not, Soren," I answer confidently. "I gave it a lot of thought, and it was a difficult decision. But I think it's the right decision for me and my family."

"Well, then. I suppose we have work to do in these next two months. Why don't we discuss your report?" he says.

"Of course," I reply. "Here's the written report. I'll just give you the executive summary and let you read over the details later. I'll answer any questions you have today, then we'll work out any other bugs later."

I hand Soren his copy of the report. He takes it from my hand, and immediately sets it on the table, never taking his eyes off me the entire time. It feels like he isn't even interested in the report. His face wears no expression. I have no idea what he's thinking, and I feel an uncomfortable silence creeping into the room.

"As you'll see in the report, I have two major concerns," I begin. "The first is internal security. We need to make sure that everybody in the office has state-of-the-art virus scanning software on their network computers. We also need to make sure that every word processing, spreadsheet, and presentation document, as well as every email we bring into our network is scanned to filter out virus attachments. Any portable USB drives must also be scanned. We need to scan every email attachment to ensure it isn't a virus of some kind. We already have software in place, but it's out of date and the virus definitions aren't being properly updated. It's going to cost a bit to get everybody's machine up to date, but compared to the cost of a network crash, the price is small. Any questions so far?"

"No. You've been quite thorough," he says, his voice sounding emotionally flat. "Go on."

"As I mentioned at the last meeting, my biggest concern is preventing hackers from penetrating our network. I'm talking about individual hackers, or a Botnet that hackers could turn against our website. This would potentially allow them to steal personal information about network users and church members, or even create a Dedicated Denial of Service — a DDOS — that could crash our network and bring our Ministry to its knees for days. We need to buy some more expensive software that scans continuously for attacks on our server's ports."

"Of course, my dear. And your recommendations are in the report?" he says, almost flippantly.

"Yes," I answer. "Do you have any questions?"

"Only one. You demonstrated quite successfully at our last meeting how somebody could set up one of these Botnets to use against us. Could we not set up a similar Botnet, but use it for good, rather than evil? We could learn about church members, their attitudes, the demographics of people who give to our Ministries. Do you see what I mean?"

Okay, here it comes. He's going to ask me to create a Botnet. Tell him why he doesn't need one.

"Yes, I do. But you don't need a Botnet to do that. All you need to do is to use *Cookies* — little applets that ask users if we can collect very limited, specific types of information. It's simple, and most websites use them these days."

"I see. But I'd still like you to create a Botnet for me, Angela. I see many future applications for having one that is controlled by our network."

"I'm… I'm afraid I can't do that," I stutter. "It's illegal. We can't go inserting Trojans on people's computers without their consent."

"Is it now?" Soren says flatly. "I'm afraid I'm quite surprised by your attitude today. Just last month, you were so excited about being in New York. You were going to consider my offer to come with me on some of my Ministries. And you were so very excited about learning how to hack into networks. Now, suddenly, that has all changed. Can you tell me why everything has changed so suddenly, Angela?"

I feel Soren's eyes burning into me like lasers. His cold, emotionless voice gives me the shivers. Alarm bells are ringing in my mind. My plan isn't working. I'm on the defensive now, trying to salvage a way to break free from a vise that is methodically closing its jaws on me.

"Soren, you gave me the job of beefing up the security of the WWCC network. And I'm fully dedicated to doing that for you in the next two months. If you want to build a Botnet after that, I'm sure you can hire somebody else to step into my shoes after I leave New York."

A smile starts to return to Soren's face, but I don't like the looks of it — it's more of a smirk than a smile, and it feels creepy.

"Angela, my dear. I'm afraid I can't accept your resignation. I've become much too fond of you to let you go."

At that moment, he gently tips my chin up so that I can't avoid his eyes. I see the look of infatuation in them, and immediately I start feeling apprehensive about where this is heading. Before I know it, he's leaning forward, giving me a soft kiss on my lips. He undoes the top two buttons on my blouse, exposing my cleavage. I see his eyes roaming over the round curves of my breasts, then his hand slowly caresses them as they roam over the outside of my blouse My body freezes, taken completely by surprise. At the same time, my mind goes numb — the last remnants of my plan vaporize, leaving me at a complete loss for words. I feel my heart pumping, my body tensing, and my hands perspiring. My brain cells start scrambling for a new solution.

Soren looks me directly in the eyes and stares me down.

"Your sudden change of heart wouldn't have anything to do with the accounting questions you had about the church's real estate arm, would it? It seems like such a coincidence that you seemed to lose your enthusiasm after you questioned me about that. Be honest with me, Angela. Have you been a bad girl and gone looking in places where you shouldn't be looking?"

I feel my heart pounding like a locomotive, and my chest is so tight I can hardly breathe. He knows he's got me. I've never been able to lie, ever since the day I decided that a Crayola mural would be a terrific idea for my bedroom wall, trying to convince Momma and Papa that the infamous *nobody* did it. I feel myself taking a giant swallow.

"I won't tell anybody, Soren. It's none of my business. Nobody needs to know," I whimper.

"That's where you're mistaken, Angela. It *wasn't* any of your business. But now that you know, you are *part* of that business. If anybody ever questions me, I'll be sure to let them know that the real estate books are *your* accounting responsibility. We're both in this together — you and me — if anything happens to me, it happens to you. Do I make myself clear?"

I gulp again. *Crystal clear*. My mind floats somewhere else for an instant. Then I'm aware that Soren is talking to me again.

"… so, you will continue working on network security, and you will build me a Botnet at the same time." He smiles another creepy, artificial smile at me. "And I'm so looking forward to having you come with me on some of my Ministries, if you know what I mean."

A shiver travels down the entire length of my spine. I have a pretty good idea what he means.

"You can move the children to New York, or leave them in Cleveland, if you like," he says. His voice is cold and emotionless. "If you move them here, I'll help you pay for someone to look after them when we're on the road together. But I really can't allow you to leave me, my dear. I'm afraid you belong to me now, so I suggest that you make the best of our new relationship and decide what you would like to do. It would be so unfortunate if you made the wrong choice and something happened to those two beautiful children, wouldn't it?"

There it is. Too late, I realize that I'm trapped in something that is far bigger than I ever imagined, and I'm in way over my head. I need to buy myself some time to tread water and to think.

"Of course," I reply. "Under the circumstances, I suppose I can reconsider my decision."

Soren's face immediately brightens, as if nothing had happened.

"That's my girl!" he exclaims. "I knew you'd see things my way. So it's agreed. You'll continue working on network security, but you'll also start working on building a Botnet for me. I think we should stay in much closer contact until I'm back in New York, so you'll need to have my cell number. When I'm back next month, we can go out for a night on the town to celebrate! How would you like that?"

Soren is interrupted by the ringing of the phone on his desk. A frown appears on his forehead and he pauses, apparently deciding whether to answer or not. He huffs, then hits the intercom button.

"Yes, Jeanette, what is it?" he asks, the tone of his voice displaying his displeasure at being interrupted.

"Ms. Marshall the reporter, is here for the interview," the secretary replies.

Soren takes a quick glance at the Rolex on his wrist. Much to my relief, he looks surprised. I'm hoping he decides to end our meeting.

"Oh… right," he says. "Tell her I'll be with her shortly. Thanks, Jeanette." He hangs up the phone, then pauses for a moment, thinking. Then he looks at me again, his face breaking into a smile again.

"There's something else I'd like you to do for me," he says. "There's a young lady outside — a freelance journalist — who wants to do an article about the church. Of course, I'll be spending the next hour with her. But I think she needs to talk with someone like you, Angela. Somebody who is a Believer, and somebody who loves working for the church as well. Perhaps you two could go for lunch together — on me, of course."

Soren frowns and his eyes narrow, suddenly becoming serious again. "You will do that for me, won't you, Angela?"

I look into his eyes and realize he won't take no for an answer. I open my mouth to speak, but my mouth and throat are dry and nothing emerges. I clear my throat and swallow. "Of course. I'll be happy to talk with her," I answer, trying my best to be convincing.

"Wonderful! Thank you, my dear. Now, where were we?"… Ah, yes! Of course. You will be working on the Botnet. And we will be keeping in touch until I'm back next month. Then a night to remember in New York when I return!" he says triumphantly.

I realize that I need to match his level of excitement, so I feel myself putting on a mask and becoming somebody else. I'm now acutely aware that my life, and the lives of my children, depend on being convincing.

"I'd like that a lot," I answer. "I'm looking forward to it."

I paint my best fake smile on my new mask. Soren starts telling me all about his grandiose plans for the WWCC, but my mind goes into overdrive and I don't hear anything he's saying. It's now abundantly clear that I'm working for a crazy man, and I only have one month to find a way out of his manipulative grasp.

"THAT'S QUITE a story," the woman exclaims.

I'm sitting across the table from the freelance reporter, who has introduced herself as Ricki Marshall, from Las Vegas. She is an imposing, solid-looking woman — not overweight — just big boned and muscular. Her short hair is blonde and she has piercing blue eyes. Her voice is husky — still feminine, but with hint of masculinity in it.

"So you decided to take up Pastor Soren's offer," she states. "Just how did he decide to put your computer genius to work?"

I feel my stomach feeling unsettled — gurgling — my lunch isn't sitting well. My hands are fidgeting with the serviette in my lap, and I'm having difficulty looking Ricki in the eye. I have to be careful not to say anything about the church that will make her suspect Soren and his motives in any way.

"Well… uh… I started off just learning the accounting system here, and learning to find my way around the computer system. Believe it or not, I'd never used a computer for accounting before. My boss in Cleveland was old-school — everything done on paper ledgers, so it took me a while just to learn the basics."

"And then?" Ricki asks.

I clear my throat again. "Once I picked up the basics, I started learning about the church's financial structure. The WWCC is really much bigger and more complex than I had ever imagined."

"How so?" Marshall asked.

I feel my heart starting to pump harder and I feel myself getting hot.

Damn, Angela. Why did you say anything about finances? What were you thinking?

"Umh… ah…" I mutter, scrambling to find the right words. Finally, I open my mouth to answer.

"As you can imagine, because the WWCC has moved from being a small brick and mortar church to being a worldwide internet phenomenon, the church brings in money in a number of ways. There's the cash offerings from the original church in Victoria, online donations and offerings. And now there's tickets for his Ministry and merchandise that followers can buy at his Ministry shows, and even online."

"Can you give me any idea how much the church is bringing in?" Ricki says.

I feel immediate panic. My heart starts racing and my chest is tight. I feel my hands shaking and I make sure to keep them in my lap so Marshall doesn't see them.

"You know I can't reveal that, Ms. Marshall," I say politely, hoping she'll take the hint that she's crossed a boundary. I take a quick look at her. She's studying me.

"Well, the WWCC must be doing pretty well," Ricki states. "I've heard rumors that Pastor Soren is starting to buy up real estate. Not just in North America, either. I'm hearing rumors of South America and Europe too. He's been seen having meetings with real estate people in California and around Las Vegas. Can you comment on that?"

Ricki's reference to South American has me shaken. I can't stop thinking about my recent discoveries — the river of money flowing into the church from Soren's shady Asian enterprises — the irregularities in online donations. I feel my ears getting hot, then my face. I'm starting to blush, so I look away.

"All I can tell you, Ms. Marshall, is that the church is thriving, and Pastor Soren is looking for ways to spread his word, and to expand the church's popularity base." I take a quick glance at Marshall and see the woman eyeing me. I look down at my lap.

"Ms. Baranyi… Angela…is there something wrong. You look like you're scared. Is it something about the church… or Pastor Soren?"

"No!" I blurt, trying to be convincing. "It's nothing like that. I've just got a lot on my plate right now — being away from my kids, family, and friends in Cleveland. It's hard." I feel real tears starting to form in my eyes. I feel Marshall's hand on mine. It feels completely different than Soren's touch. It feels warm and full of compassion.

"You're sure?" Marshall asks. I wipe the tears from my eyes and force myself to look at her face.

"I'm sure," I repeat. "Are you married? Do you have kids back in Las Vegas?"

"No," she replies. "Not married… no kids. It's pretty hard to be married and to be a freelance journalist at the same time. I have to be ready to hop on a plane and follow the news, wherever it happens. You learn to make a lot of sacrifices for this job. I have good friends when I'm back in Vegas. That's enough for me right now."

I look at Marshall's face and realize we're not so different. We both know what it's like to make sacrifices. I realize I like the woman, and I'd like to open up to her. But I can't. What she doesn't know, and what I can't tell her, is just how big my sacrifice is going to be.

"Look, Ms. Marshall, I want you to know that I'm so grateful to Pastor Soren for offering me this job and taking me into the church. If it was in my hometown, it would truly be the opportunity of a lifetime. I'm just struggling with trying to decide if I belong here in New York. That's all."

I see Marshall studying me. Probably deciding whether to keep pressing for more information or to let it go. She glances at her watch, then picks up her voice recorder and shuts it off. "I think I've got what I need," she says. "No more questions. Let's enjoy what's left of your lunch hour."

I feel like I've just dodged a bullet, managing to convince Marshall that my problems are personal — nothing to do with the WWCC. I manage to relax and we start talking about Cleveland, and then about her life in Las Vegas. By the time lunch is finished and we say goodbye, I'm confident that I won't have to deal with Ricki Marshall's questions again.

I realize that my lunch with Marshall was a short-lived reprieve from my dilemma. Now I have to find the confidence to find a way to keep my children safe, and to leave the WWCC and Soren Kristiansen behind me for good.

I feel tension creeping back into my body again, and I feel my heart pounding. A tension headache is starting to build, like the ominous black clouds of a summer storm. I still don't have a plan, and I'm running out of time.

CHAPTER 6

IT'S ONLY ten a.m., but the apartment is heating up and I'm already starting to feel my clothes clinging to my skin. It's going to be another hot, hazy, and humid June day. My fingers tap away frantically on my laptop, setting up the last of my intricate web of bank accounts. Time is running out. I only have a matter of a few short days before Soren is back in New York, and I have no doubts that he expects to wine, dine, and take me to bed. I shift my focus back to the task at hand, adding the username and password to the long list of account information I've stored, and then I close and lock the file.

Getting Soren's bank accounts and passwords, and all of his underworld contacts has been mere child's play, now that I have a clone of his laptop. He had all of the contact information for his bank account in Geneva. And I discovered he'd contacted somebody to get new identities made for himself. I only wish I knew if he'd followed through. If he had a new identity, he hadn't left any trace on his laptop… yet.

So much for finances. Now for the tricky part of the plan.

I pick up my cell phone and open a new text message to Soren. He's been keeping close tabs on me since the last meeting, sending numerous text messages and emails. He even phoned me several times. I've responded to each one of them, trying to sound more compliant and enthusiastic each time. I've given him regular updates on my network security project and the Botnet development.

The reports are all false, of course. I've been devoting every waking minute to my escape, only going into the WWCC often enough to convince people that my latest project requires me to work from home, outside of the WWCC network.

Soren will eventually find out I've been lying. But by then, it really won't matter, will it?

I pause before typing the text, making sure of exactly how I want to word it. Satisfied with the message I've composed in my mind, my thumbs go into action.

I'm ashamed to admit something to you. I hope God will forgive me. I still feel the shiver from your hand on my breasts. I can't stop thinking about it. I need to feel you touching them and holding them in your warm hands. I can't wait for Saturday night.

That should do it. A couple more texts like that over the next week should have him hooked. Not too seductive, and lots of guilt thrown in for good measure. For my plan to work, I have to seem totally believable to Soren. If I can appeal to the head on his penis this week, maybe the head on his shoulders will lose its ability for critical thinking.

I go through the checklist in my mind. Bank accounts. Check. Text message to Soren. Check. Next item on list — sexy new dress. I can go shopping for that tomorrow. My eyes fall on the next item — dependable used car. That's a bit more complicated. I don't have much experience in that department. I decide I'd better make good use of my Saturday and do some car shopping.

My new disposable cell phone rings and I notice it's an unknown number. I put down my old personal cell phone to answer the disposable one.

"Hello," I answer.

"This is Rafael. The papers you wanted, they are done. Do you have the money?"

I won't have any money after I'm finished with you, you crook! I've had to use half of my savings. Your fake ID's had better be really good.

"Yes," I answer.

"Meet me at the Bow Bridge in the park tomorrow at noon. I'll be wearing a Knicks jersey and cap. Have the cash in a backpack. Any questions?"

I can't lie. The adrenaline starts kicking in, and I'm starting to feel a bit like a Bond girl.

"I'll be there," I answer. Rafael ends the call abruptly and the untraceable phone goes dead in my hand. I stare at the device, hardly able to believe what I've gotten myself into.

My emotions are all over the place. Excitement and adrenaline at the prospect of being free from Soren. Fear at the prospect of having him catch me. And worst of all, a terrible sense of sadness, loss, and guilt. But will I ever be able to convince myself that I have to leave Julia and Nicholas, perhaps for the rest of my life, to keep them safe?

I TAKE ONE last look in the mirror to make sure I'm not going to have any wardrobe malfunctions with my outlandish new designer dress. I mean, outlandish for me. I feel half naked when I walk, the broad slit up the right side of the sleek white gown allowing a definite breeze to blow over my legs and up my thighs. I look over my shoulder at the plunging back line, just barely seeing the beginnings of a separation at the top of my backside. Turning my body, I still can't believe I'm looking at myself when I see the gown's plunging neckline. The strategically placed silver sparkles ensure that nobody sees any nipple. I'm placing all of my faith in the sticky tape that's supposed to keep the sheer fabric from lifting away from my breasts, to keep from exposing them for the entire world to see.

He's going to have a lot of trouble keeping his hands away from this! Remember, Angela. You need to tease him — give him enough of a taste to make sure he thinks there's going to be a next time.

The intercom buzzes.

"Angela, it's Soren. I'm waiting downstairs, but no need to rush. We have plenty of time."

I look at my watch and reach for the small silver clutch.

It's showtime!

I lock the apartment door, and then ride the elevator to the lobby, taking deep breaths and slowly gaining confidence as I gaze at my reflection in the mirror beside me. I see a strong, sexy, independent-looking blonde woman.

As I emerge from the elevator, I see Soren holding the passenger door of his sleek, black Mercedes open for me. Dressed in a black tuxedo, he is definite eye candy for the ladies and he knows it. I just know him too well to fall for that. He reaches for my hand and raises it to his lips, giving it the lightest of kisses.

"You're stunning, my dear," he says. His eyes lock onto the gaping valley between my breasts. He is temporarily lost for words.

Awesome! He can't take his eyes off the girls.

"Thank you," I reply demurely. "You're looking pretty dapper yourself, Pastor." His face breaks into a broad smile, realizing how much attention we are likely to attract tonight. It doesn't seem to trouble him that he is going to be seen in public with somebody other than his wife, Anika Kristiansen. The image of the photograph in Soren's office flashes through my consciousness, and I feel a fleeting moment of guilt. I tell myself this is all for show. Although he doesn't know it, I need to attract attention even more than he does.

Soren closes my door, then walks around the Mercedes and slides behind the wheel.

"I have a treat for you tonight," he announces. "I'm taking you to *Le Bernardin*. It has the finest seafood in all of New York. I hope you enjoy it."

"I'm sure I will," I answer, knowing it's probably the last four-star restaurant meal I'll be eating in public for a long, long time.

I'M HAVING a difficult time keeping focused on my plan. The evening has had far too many distractions, which on any other night would be welcome.

"I can't believe I met both Regis Philbin and Donald Trump!" I exclaim. "And the food! It's unbelievable. I'm going to have a hard time eating spaghetti and meatballs in my boring apartment after this."

"You won't have to… at least, not for the next week," Soren reminds me. "Don't forget, you'll be joining me in Oklahoma City after your two days in Cleveland. Then we'll be together in Dallas and Houston before I have to fly back to Victoria."

"You're right," I say. "I feel spoiled already. You're being far too good to me."

"Nonsense, my dear. Now that we've reached an… understanding… about our relationship, nothing is too good for you."

Soren is seated to my right, and we're both partially hidden from view, since we're seated at the back of the restaurant. Soren slides his hand under the table and onto my thigh. Initially, my body tenses. I have to tell it to relax. I look at Soren and give him a coy smile, signaling that I'm up for a bit of sex play. He continues to talk about nothing important, the tips of his fingers exploring into my freshly-waxed nether regions, completely unencumbered by underwear. I see the corners of his mouth turn up and his eyebrows rise, as he discovers this pleasant surprise. I take his hand in mind and give it an affectionate squeeze, holding it in mine for a minute before returning it to his own lap. As I do, I manage to brush his crotch with my fingertips, finding that it's already rising to the occasion. I flash him a knowing smile.

"Since you have to catch an early flight to Cleveland in the morning, and we don't have time for a show, what do you say to going back to my place for a nightcap?" Soren says.

"Any other night, I'd like that," I lie. "But if I go to your place, you know I might want to stay all night, and I can't do that tonight. We'll have each other to ourselves in three or four days. Can you wait for me?" I ask. I make sure to brush his hard penis with my fingertips one more time, just so he knows what he has to look forward to.

"Barely," he says. "I don't think I've ever wanted anybody this much." Judging from how hard his penis is becoming, I believe him. "I must say I'm disappointed in you, Angela. I thought we had reached an understanding about what you owe me. I really thought that you might come back to my apartment with me."

I squeeze his hand and gaze into his eyes, sending subliminal messages to his brain.

"I'm looking forward to going away and being with you, Soren. Do you have any idea how long it's been since I've been with a man?" I lie. "We can sleep late and make love every morning while after we're together."

I kiss him softly on his lips, letting mine linger long enough for him to get a good taste, and to want more.

"But I really must get home early tonight. I have to be at LaGuardia by six o'clock tomorrow morning for my flight to Cleveland. Can you forgive me if I ask you to call it an early night?"

"I suppose," Soren pouts. But then, just as quickly, his smiling mask reappears. Once again putting on a happy face for all to see, he signals for our check.

SOREN PARKS the Mercedes on the street, a couple of doors away from my apartment. The street is dark. I take his hand in mine, signaling that I don't want him to get out of the car yet.

"I had a wonderful time, Soren," I say. "Thank you for such an incomparable dining experience. I've never had seafood like that before."

"I told you," Soren says, wearing a look of pride. "It's a sensory journey. The texture of that barely-cooked fish on your tongue… and its exquisite taste… it's almost orgasmic."

"I like that description," I say. I catch him by surprise, leaning towards him and placing my lips over his. I start teasing his lips with my tongue, encouraging him to open them so I can explore and tease inside his mouth. Just as he starts to explore back with his tongue, I pull my lips away.

"I know something else that would feel orgasmic in your mouth," I whisper.

I guide his hand under my dress to my perfectly smooth nether regions, and Soren immediately gets the message. He starts kissing me slowly, sensually, and expertly before he starts an agonizingly methodical tease of my genital area. He's good, I have to admit it. I feel his hands working their way under my gown, and I gasp as he tears off the tape that holds the gown close to my breasts. He is kneading them and teasing my nipples. But I close my eyes, imagining that it's somebody other than Soren who is ravaging me — the lover of my fantasies. My arousal continues to build.

Soren guides my body into a reclining position on the front seat of the luxury Mercedes. He spreads the flaps of my gown and spreads my legs apart. Then I feel what I can't deny that I've been longing to feel — my fantasy lover's lips and tongue working their way around my thighs, teasing me until I can't stand it anymore. I moan as his tongue finds my clitoris and he teases it with light flicks. Then I feel his tongue parting my labia, exploring inside. My juices are flowing freely, like a springtime thaw. It feels so good. It's been so long. I feel the tension continuing to build inside.

"Come on, Soren… harder!" I moan. I'm pushing myself against his face and grinding as fast as I can. I can't make myself come quickly enough. Suddenly, I feel the tension explode inside. I feel jets of liquid squirting from me, all over Soren's shocked face. Judging from his surprised expression, I don't think he's ever encountered female ejaculation before. I touch the car seat beneath my bottom and feel my fluids all over the leather. My rapid breathing begins to slow, and I gradually gather my composure. I sit up and guide his head back towards mine, kissing him on the lips, savoring the sweet, salty taste of my secretions lingering there.

Then I push Soren back into his seat. My hand drops into his lap and my fingers find his rock-hard penis.

"My turn to feel something orgasmic in my mouth," I whisper in his ear. "A little something to keep you going for the next few days."

I grab his cock, still inside his trousers, and squeeze tightly.

"Ohhhh," he moans. My fingers find his belt and undo it. Then they find and lower his fly and unfasten his pants, revealing a large tent inside his boxers.

"Move back to give me more room," I command.

Soren slides back against his door, as far as he can go. As he does, my fingers free his erection from his boxers, and I lean over so my head is in his lap. I've never enjoyed giving head before, but tonight it's a necessity. My tongue goes to work, teasing his head and rim, then flicking at the sweet spots on his shaft. As I go to work on his cock, I find my purse and open it with one hand, removing my cell phone. I transfer it to my left hand, and casually deposit it on the floor behind Soren's seat.

"Oh, my God," he moans, not realizing the humor in his words as I give a blow job to the Pastor of the *World-Wide Community of Christ*. I feel the pace of Soren's breathing quicken, and I feel him thrusting back, deeper into the back of my throat. I feel him tense. I release his throbbing cock from my mouth, just as he spurts a jet of semen.

"Nooooo…" he moans. He grabs my hair and jerks my head back down towards his spewing cock. My nose slams into the steering wheel and I yelp with pain. I feel, a warm, salty fluid under my nose and on my upper lip. At first I think it's semen, but then I realize it's blood. Damn! My nose is bleeding all over everything. I wipe the semen and blood away from my nose with my hand. Then I plop my butt back down in my seat, tilting my head back. My hand, covered in blood and semen, feels the pool of vaginal fluid on the car seat from my own orgasm.

"Are you okay?" Soren asks, a little too late.

Suddenly, I start laughing. My hand has found the car seat, drenched in assorted body fluids. Soren pauses, not knowing what to think, then he starts laughing too.

"Are we getting old when we start injuring ourselves while having sex in a car?"

I can't stop laughing at the absurd perfection of this moment, knowing that Soren won't ever understand why I find it so funny.

… Until it's too late.

HAVING FINALLY convinced Soren that I'm okay, we dress ourselves. He walks around the Mercedes to be a gentleman and helps me climb out of the low, sporty car. I smooth out the gown as best I can, and he escorts me into my building, up to the elevator.

"I'm okay from here," I assure him. "Thank you for seeing me inside, and thank you for a most enjoyable evening." I smile a genuine smile. Not because I found the entire evening to be pleasurable, but because my plan unfolded better than I could possibly have imagined. I kiss him fully on the lips. He has no idea that it's his goodbye kiss.

The elevator door opens, I let go of his hand, and I walk through the door, turning to give him a little wave as it closes. I press the button for the fourth floor, waiting for the door to close. As it does, it finally brings down the curtain on my performance. I feel a jerk as the elevator begins its slow ascent. At the same time, I let out an enormous sigh of relief.

Stage one complete — now for stage two!

I rush from the elevator and down the hallway to my apartment. Finding my key in the tiny clutch purse, my shaky hands fumble to insert it into the lock. A small carry-on suitcase and a briefcase with my brand new personal laptop computer are waiting for me, just inside the door. Without turning on the light, and after making sure that nobody sees me, I grab the handles of both objects and carry them into the hallway. I lock the door behind me, leaving all of my remaining belongings, including my WWCC laptop, behind in the apartment.

To avoid making noise, I haul the carry-on bag and briefcase to the stairwell in my arms. Still in my evening gown, I take the stairs down to the main floor. I walk through the garbage room to the rear exit of the building, closing the heavy steel door carefully behind me. Even though I've checked the alley to make sure there aren't any security cameras, I wait for my eyes to adjust to the dark, then I venture tentatively into the alley, keeping to the shadows for about fifty yards until I come to a large dumpster. I conceal myself behind one end of the dumpster, making sure that I'm not visible from any apartment windows. I remove the contents from my small clutch and toss it into the dumpster.

I take a furtive look around to make sure I'm
still alone. Once I'm sure, I peel the evening gown,
stained with a mixture of Soren's and my body
fluids, from my body. As it sails into the dumpster, I
find myself standing completely naked and
vulnerable in the alley. Quickly, I retrieve a pair of
blue jeans from the top of the carry-on bag and pull
them over my hips and my bare ass. After
impatiently donning a bra, I grab a t-shirt and a pair
of sandals, I close the zipper on the carry-on bag
and I'm ready to go. With the laptop case swung
over my shoulder, I pick up the carry-on bag and
walk quickly down the alley to East 10th. Finally, I
feel like I'm far enough from home to put the carry-
on bag down on its wheels. A quick walk takes me
to the parking garage on East 11th, where I've
parked my recent purchase: an old '94 Honda Civic.
I throw my luggage in the trunk, then I remove the
backpack that I've pre-packed with food, cash, and
my old and new ID's. Satisfied that nobody is
watching me, I hop into the vehicle.

Before long, I'm through the Lincoln Tunnel,
heading west on the New Jersey Turnpike through
Newark. My sights are set on the Poconos, then
I-81 to Syracuse. I look at my watch, noticing that
it's almost midnight. I finally allow my body to
relax a bit. I just need to be in Toronto in time to
catch the afternoon Swissair Flight that gets me into
Geneva on Monday morning. I figure I'll be in

Syracuse by about four a.m., and hopefully across the Canadian border and at Pearson Airport in Toronto by nine a.m. I keep a careful eye on the speedometer, keeping my new fake driver's license and passport on the passenger seat beside me, just in case. Feeling some remaining tension in my shoulders, I take a long, deep breath, and then I let it out slowly.

For a fleeting moment, I feel free — as if a huge weight has just been taken off my shoulders. Then the feeling is gone — replaced by a crushing feeling of guilt and sadness at what I'm doing as reality hits me. I'm leaving my old life as Angela Baranyi behind, including everybody I love and cherish: Julia and Nicholas, Momma and Papa, and Dori, who has been like a sister to me. Will they ever know what happened to me? Will they ever forgive me? Tears start streaming from my eyes and down both cheeks, my nose sniffling. I keep blinking the tears away so I can see the highway through the watery haze. I keep telling myself that I'm doing it to keep them safe. But I'm wondering if I'll ever convince myself enough to believe it.

CHAPTER 7

I HEAVE a huge sigh of relief as I drive away from Canada Customs and Immigration in Fort Erie. I've officially become Anna Benz. My new passport didn't raise any eyebrows with Agent Oulette, a friendly woman who wished me a cheery "have a good night, eh", as she passed my passport back to me. My story about staying with friends in Amherst on the weekend, then flying to meet my parents in Switzerland wasn't questioned.

I look at my watch. Seven forty-five a.m. on Sunday. I've made good time and should be at the airport in Toronto right on schedule. I desperately need to find a Ladies' room so I can freshen up after last night's events. Then I need to close my eyes for a while. As I approach Niagara Falls, Ontario, I see the sign for services and I decide to make a quick pit stop. I fill up a reusable Starbucks thermos with its Canadian counterpart, Tim Horton's coffee. The smell of fresh java and breakfast sandwiches greets me as I enter, making me realize just how hungry I am. I decide I can spare ten minutes to put some food in my stomach before I venture out on the

QEW — the Queen Elizabeth Way — for the last leg of my drive into Toronto.

The view of Lake Ontario and the Welland Canal is stunning in the early-morning June sunshine. There isn't a cloud in the sky — only a grey haze on the horizon leading to Toronto, my destination. Traffic is light as I sip my coffee and start reviewing my plan. I'll need to freshen up and change into my suit when I arrive in Geneva. My blue jeans and scruffy appearance would surely raise suspicion in the elite banking establishments of Switzerland. My expensive suit, and the handful of business cards that I had printed in New York, should put the finishing touches on my new professional identities as two separate real estate developers. The tricky part will be making sure I remember to keep my two new roles separate and convincing.

My mind continues to obsess over my plans as I ascend the skyway and see the port and industrial heart of Hamilton on my left, and the city of Burlington on my right. Shortly after I descend from the massive skyway, the highway veers right for the final leg of my journey into Toronto. I can barely make out the ghostly outline of skyscrapers and the CN Tower in the distance, as my old Civic hums obediently along the QEW towards Pearson International Airport.

I run through a number of different versions of the email I'll send to Soren on Monday. None of the versions feels quite right. I'm hoping that a few hours of sleep on the flight to Europe will sharpen my synapses and help me find what I really want to say to him. I only have one chance. The safety of my parents and my children depends on making my message crystal clear.

I WALK up the ramp from the aircraft and into Geneva International Airport. As I reach the concourse, on the way to immigration, I look out through the windows at a dreary grey day, perfect for how I'm feeling after only a couple of fitful naps on the flight from Toronto. My overnight drive from New York and my lack of sleep on the plane is catching up with me. I need to find a toilet to freshen up. Then I need coffee to clear my head before I check into my hotel. The next four hours, and my appointments at two Swiss Banks, are critical if I'm going to pull this caper off. I can't afford to make a single mistake.

I arrive at immigration and hand my passport to Agent Jeanneret, a surly-looking man who looks like he can't wait to finish his shift. Unlike Agent Oulette at the Canadian Border, Monsieur Jeanneret is all business.

"Madame Benz, the reason for your visit to Switzerland?" he asks. I try to look weary, which isn't much of a stretch. "Business. I'm a real estate developer. I'm here for meetings."

"And who are you meeting with?" he asks.

"The Richard Group," I answer. "They build nursing and long-term care homes for the elderly."

Good thing I did my homework!

Jeanneret looks closely at my passport, then at me again, then back at the passport. His fingers type something into his computer and he stares at the screen. Suddenly, it feels like the only thing I can hear is the beating of my heart.

"This is a new passport?" he asks.

This is it. I'm finished now. How long will I get for travelling on a forged U.S. Passport?

"Yes… yes, it is," I mumble.

"You forgot to sign it, Madame. Do you have any other identification on you?"

Stupid me! I can't believe Oulette didn't notice that in Canada!

"I'm sorry!" I mutter. "How stupid of me. Of course, I've got my driver's license."

I scrounge around in my purse for my new fake license. Jeanneret hands me the passport.

"Sign please," he commands, watching me closely as I sign the document. I try to avoid holding my breath as I wait for him to compare the signature on my driver's license with the sample I'd just provided. He looks up at me over the rim of his glasses.

"Have a nice visit, Madame," he says, passing my documents back to me. I give him a weary smile.

"Thank you," I reply, not wishing to show how grateful I really was.

I follow the throng of humanity out into the main terminal, looking to meet my three biggest needs at this moment — a toilet, a cellular shop where I can buy a pre-paid phone, and someplace to find a coffee and some food. I let out a long sigh as I look around the terminal.

So far, so good. Two hurdles down — getting into Canada and Switzerland as Anna Benz.

But those two hurdles are nothing compared to the two I have to clear in the next three hours.

I CLIMB into a second cab, on the second leg of my short journey to the Astoria Hotel. Maybe I'm just being paranoid, but I don't want people to notice me while I'm here in Geneva. And if they do, I don't want to make it easy for them to find me. I flip open my new pre-paid phone and I enter the phone number for the cab company into the phone's contact list, followed by the numbers of the two banks I'll be visiting in the next couple of hours.

I lean back in the rear seat and start rehearsing the scripts I've written in my mind, making sure to get myself in character for each script. If I'm going to be pretending to be two different people, I'd better make each of them convincing. I realize I can't afford to make a single mistake that will raise any suspicions. Everything I've planned will be for nothing if either bank feels the need to freeze the funds for a week, or to look into my background.

I notice the Cornavin train station on my left, just as the cab slows down in front of my destination, the Hotel Astoria. The hotel's grey stucco exterior is ordinary and unimposing — ideal for my purposes. After tipping my driver, I wheel my carry-on bag, with its meagre contents, to the front desk.

"Hello. You should have a reservation for three nights for Anna Benz, beginning last night. I'm assuming my room was held so I could check in this morning."

"Bonjour, Madame Benz," says the desk clerk, a young woman with dark hair bundled into a ponytail. "Let me see…,"

"It is early, Madame," she says. "You will have to wait until we are able to clean a room for you."

I feel my temperature rising and my heart pounding. My hands feel clammy.

"I'm sorry, Miss," I reply. "I paid for last night so my room would be available this morning so I can prepare for important business meetings. Would you please check again? I'm sure you'll find that you have an open room for me."

The young woman's fingers click away on her keyboard and she stares into her monitor. The longer she stares, the greater sense of panic I feel.

I need to have a shower, wash my hair, and get some makeup on my face. I can't look like this if I'm supposed to be a real estate investor!

A middle-aged man with greying hair and a dark navy suit appears from the room behind the desk and notices the puzzled look on the desk clerk's face. The badge on his suit says *H. LeClerc*.

"Is there a problem, Madeleine?" he says to the desk clerk. She breaks into rapid French and points to her monitor as she explains her dilemma. He points to something on the screen and asks her to type some commands on her keyboard.

"I apologize for the delay, Madame Benz," he says. "I had to show Madeleine how to look up yesterday's reservation screen. She has only started working here. Your room is ready, as you requested."

I feel a weight lifting from my shoulders and my heart begins to slow as I let out a long breath. My temperature feels like it's returning to normal and my hands gradually feel less clammy.

"Thank you," I sigh gratefully.

"Here is your key, Madame. You are on the second floor. Do you need help with your bags?"

"No, thank you, Monsieur," I reply. "You've been most helpful. Is there an iron in my room? I'm afraid my business clothes may not look their best after being in this small bag. I need to be ready for a meeting in an hour."

"No, Madame, but I will bring it to your room personally. I should only be a few minutes," he explains.

"Thank you," I reply, reaching for the handle on my carry-on bag, and heading towards the lift.

Okay, Angela. Time to perform miracles in minutes. I take another deep breath, digging deep for the energy I need for this morning.

I rush from the lift on the second floor, breaking into a jog and glancing at the passing room numbers until I come to my room. As I insert my key in the slot, the green light flashes, followed by a '*click*' from the lock as it releases. I throw the door open and go into action, dragging the carry-on bag across the floor and up onto the bed in one smooth motion. I take my suit and blouse from the small bag, frowning at some obvious wrinkles, and lay them out on the bed. Looking for a closet, I find some hangers for hanging my ensemble. I swing open the bathroom door and hang my suit and blouse on the inside of the door.

I hear a knock on my door. True to his word, Monsieur LeClerc leaves me an iron and points out that there is a small ironing board in the closet.

Once the door is closed and I'm alone, I reach for my laptop and start it booting. It seems to take an eternity while I wait, totally at the mercy of the machine's hard drive and processor, which both seem to take their sweet time clicking and whirring into action. I notice myself fidgeting, tapping my foot impatiently while I wait. My entire plan depends on whether a complex chain of events had executed over the weekend. Wondering whether it occurred, or not, has been driving me crazy while I've been in transit over the Atlantic and Europe. Finally, my desktop opens for me, and I click open my web browser. I log into the account of Grace Wagner at the Swiss Bank, Lombard Odier & Cie, and then I click on the tab to show my accounts.

And there it is! I can hardly believe my eyes — a positive bank balance. The complicated web of electronic financial transactions has executed without a hitch, depositing funds into Grace Wagner's account, just as I've planned.

I run into the bathroom and start running the water for a shower, making sure to fill the bathroom with steam for letting the wrinkles out of my suit. While I'm waiting, I set up the ironing board, then I strip my two-day-old clothing from my grateful body. I step into the hot shower and allow myself a short-lived sigh of relaxation. It's all the time I can afford. I reach for the shampoo and spring back into action.

AT NINE FIFTY-SEVEN A.M., I walk through the ornate front door of Lombard Odier & Cie at 11 Rue de la Corraterie. The warm, late summer air is rejuvenating and it's a relief to breathe in the fragrances of summer after travelling for two days. The stately stone building, with its black wrought iron bars over the exterior windows, and its conservative atmosphere, reminds me of the business at hand. I straighten my shoulders and inhale deeply, feeling my confidence build. I approach the receptionist as I enter the grand stone interior of one of Switzerland's oldest, most reputable banking establishments. I pause momentarily to get into character.

"My name is Grace Wagner. I have an appointment at ten o'clock with Monsieur Foumer."

"Thank you, Madame, I will tell him you are here. Please have a seat."

I take a seat and survey my surroundings as I rehearse my script one last time. Even though the old stone building is air conditioned, it still has a faint scent of days gone by — old wood and leather. Despite the building having so much stone construction, the interior feels surprising warm and inviting as the color of the stone is a light brown shade. I hear the sharp tapping of leather shoes on the stone floors and look up to see a slender young man approaching. His hand extends as he arrives in front of me. His eyes are warm and friendly, but also sharp and focused. I remind myself not to let my guard down.

Don't trust anyone.

"Madame Wagner. I am Didier Foumer. Pleased to meet you, and welcome to Geneva. Are you enjoying your stay?" he asks.

"I'm afraid I've only just landed this morning," I say, chuckling. "But I'm looking forward to enjoying the city after my meetings are finished."

"Ah, I see," he answers. "There is much to see, and it would be a shame if you came all this way without staying for a while. Would you like to come with me?"

Monsieur Foumer ushers me into his small office and offers me a chair opposite his desk. I notice my letter to the bank sitting on his desk.

"So, Madame. You are financing some real estate developments?"

"Yes. As you can see in my letter, I represent a number of New York investors who are investing their money with a firm by the name of Anna Benz Investments. Ms. Benz is helping to finance a new project by the Richard Group, who are building a string of specialized nursing homes for elderly patients with Alzheimer's and other dementias. The buildings are planned for New York and major European cities. As I mentioned in the letter, I will be meeting with Ms. Benz today to sign the agreements, and I will need a bank draft to confirm our commitment at that time. I've confirmed that all of the investors have transferred their funds to my account in your bank."

"Certainly, Madame Wagner. I hope you understand that it is becoming more common to do electronic transfers, rather than using bank drafts, for security reasons," Foumer says. His eyes, still sharp, critically examine both my verbal and non-verbal responses.

I laugh and send a knowing smile in Monsieur Foumer's direction.

"I understand completely," I say. "But you have to know Ms. Benz. She's very 'old-school'. She likes to do things the old fashioned way. I keep trying to convince her to do more of the transactions electronically, but I'm afraid it's no use. We'll have to wait until her children manage the company someday."

We both laugh, easing the tension in the room.

"Very well, then. If you don't mind, may I see some identification? Just for security purposes," he reiterates.

I reach into my purse, where Grace Wagner's new passport is waiting, and I pass it across to

Monsieur Foumer. I feel myself getting anxious, hoping that the faint, bogus entry stamp for Amsterdam, passes inspection.

"Your passport is very new," he observes.

"Yes, I didn't realize my old one had expired. I had to get this one just before I left New York," I lied. "It would have been a catastrophe to delay my meetings with Ms. Benz."

Foumer examines my passport closely. I feel myself getting bold. I decide to break from my script.

"Would you believe I forgot to sign it before I left the U.S.?" I find myself saying. "I can't believe I was so stupid. The man at the airport told me he could have denied me entry. He was very nice and allowed me to sign it in front of him while he held my driver's license."

Foumer laughs at my story. He seems to relax when he hears that my story was accepted by Swiss Immigration.

"Do you mind if I look at your driver's license?" he asks. I pass him the fake document, grateful that my forger took the time to make my illegal licenses look like they were about two years old.

Apparently satisfied, Foumer returns my pieces of ID.

"Very well, Madame. What amount would you like me to put on the draft?"

My mouth goes dry and I find myself swallowing so I can speak.

"The full amount in the account, please — four point seven million U.S. dollars," I say, trying not to choke on the words.

Foumer raises his eyebrows for an instant.

"I will just have to get my manager to co-sign the draft. It should only take a few minutes," he says, apologetically. He shows no further reaction to the amount as he exits his office.

I try to reassure myself after he's gone.

Don't worry, Angela. Your four 4.7 million is probably small potatoes, compared to most of the transactions he sees at this bank.

But I still have a hard time believing that the poor daughter of Hungarian immigrants, a single mother of two children, now unemployed and on the run, could be walking out of this bank with a check for that amount of money. As I think of Julia and Nicholas, the heavy weight of guilt starts pressing on my shoulders again, and I feel an overwhelming sadness.

Don't cry, Angela! For God's sake, don't cry! Don't fall apart now. You're doing this for them, to keep them safe!

I wipe away the single solitary tear that barely escapes from my watery eyes, and I sniffle loudly. Then I push back my shoulders to prop up my confidence. I slow my breathing, and wait for Monsieur Foumer to return.

AN HOUR later, I emerge from the second Swiss Bank on my morning agenda, Pictet & Cie, after my short appointment. I collapse into the back seat of the taxi, feeling almost anticlimactic about what I've just done. It almost seems too easy now. I walked in and deposited 4.7 million dollars into the account of Anna Benz. The bank clerk checked my ID to ensure that I was Anna, then she deposited my check.

"Will there be anything else, Madame?"

"Nothing else, thanks."

Goodbye. That's it.

After spending two months of working feverishly to trace the inner workings of the WWCC, and then planning my own defection from Soren Kristiansen's organization, my mission is suddenly complete. The harsh reality of my life starts to sink in. I've just committed a crime and I'm a woman on the run, possibly for the rest of my life. I've left my children and parents behind for their own protection and I may never be able to see them again, without risking their safety.

I've stolen 4.7 million dollars from a man I used to admire, but now realize is a thief and an all-round sleaze bag. The good news is that he can't report me to the police without exposing his own money-laundering scheme. The bad news is that I now have to find ways to launder my own newly found wealth, and I have to hide from Soren as long as either one of us is alive.

I stuff Grace Wagner's ID into an inner pocket in my purse and zip it closed. I don't need the embarrassment of having it fall out at the airport when I'm searching for my Anna Benz ID. I'll keep Grace's ID for emergencies, but I realize that there may be a lot of people searching for Grace by the end of the day. I keep my Anna Benz ID in an easy-to-access compartment inside my purse. After all, that's who I am now — Anna Benz — thief, aspiring real estate developer, and mom-on-the-lam.

Suddenly, I feel totally exhausted. I've been running on adrenaline and I've barely slept for more than two days. I can't keep my eyes open any longer, so I tell the cabbie to wake me when we reach the Hotel Astoria.

THE HOTEL ROOM is dark when I open my eyes. I look at the room's clock and realize it's eleven o'clock. Bright light creeps into the room around the edges of the room's heavy blackout blinds. Despite having a long nap yesterday after returning from Picket & Cie, I've still slept for ten hours. I reach for the light beside the bed and wince at the sudden intrusion of light on my retinas. I rub the sleep out of my eyes and sit on the edge of the bed, wearing a blank stare on my face. The full reality of the sudden emptiness of my life hits me with full force.

What have I done?

I find myself staring right through my laptop. I was wrong about one thing after I deposited the money into Anna Benz's account at Pictet & Cie. I still have one more thing to do.

I fire up the laptop and log into my WWCC email account for the last time. I click on the icon for composing a new email message:

To: Pastor Soren Kristiansen
From: Angela Baranyi
Subject: My resignation

Pastor Soren:
It is with great regret and mixed emotions that I submit my resignation from my position at the WWCC. During the course of my employment, I discovered things about you that I wish I had never found out. I am disillusioned beyond belief that you are making money from pornography and are involved in internet scams that cheat countless honest people of their hard-earned money. For me, the final insult was when you threatened the safety

of my family if I decided against joining you in your immoral and illegal activities.

When I was at my lowest after my divorce was finalized, you and your messages of hope and faith in God became my inspiration. I still find it difficult to believe that they were all an elaborate lie. You betrayed my trust, and the trust placed in you by all of your followers. I pray that God will eventually judge you in the manner that you deserve.

By now, you might have noticed that I have liberated 4.7 million dollars from the Swiss account where your illegal income merges with the mainstream WWCC income. I like to think of that money as my insurance policy. You have my promise that I will never reveal where that money came from, and I will never report your crimes to the authorities. In return, I expect you to forget that I ever existed.

If I find out that anything bad happens to my children or parents, or if I find out that you are trying to find me or trace the money, I promise that I will report your criminal activities to the police, and I will do whatever it takes to bring you down. It's short and simple. You forget me, and I'll forget you.

Angela Baranyi.

I EMERGE from Customs and Immigration at Pearson Airport in Toronto. It's now Wednesday, four days after I diverted Soren's money from the WWCC account. I checked the internet edition of the *New York Times* yesterday. It didn't take long to find an article about a missing WWCC employee who failed to fly, as expected, from JFK to Cleveland on Sunday to visit her family back in Cleveland. I was surprised, but happy, to see that somebody had taken a picture of Soren and me together in *Le Bernardin*, perfectly capturing a moment when Soren was flirting with me.

I was even more surprised to see that the article was written by freelance journalist, Ricki Marshall, the woman who had interviewed me before I disappeared. Her article went on to say that Soren had been interviewed by police, but only as a 'person of interest' because he'd been the last person to see me. However, the article also stated that inside sources quoted police as saying that they had found my cell phone in Soren's car.

My mind is spinning, thinking about everything that's happened within the last few days. Soren must have gone crazy when they traced my phone to his car. I'll bet the crime lab guys went over the car with a fine-tooth comb. He'll have a hard time explaining all of the semen, vaginal fluids, and blood on the seats. The press will have a field day with this one — the esteemed, married, Pastor

Soren having an affair with one of his female employees. And even better, possibly being involved in her disappearance.

I take the shuttle bus to Airport Parking, then I load my luggage into the back of my faithful Civic. Before long, I'm on Highway 401, heading west. Almost immediately, I see the signs for the QEW to Niagara Falls and Buffalo. My foot twitches on the accelerator, faltering. I feel the temptation to brake and change lanes into the QEW exit. A right turn at Buffalo would take me west through New York, Pennsylvania, and Ohio to Cleveland. Maybe I could make a quick visit to explain everything to Momma and Papa. Maybe I could send them a note. They might understand.

Tears start filling my eyes. I know I'd break down if I saw Julia and Nicholas. I couldn't be that strong to say goodbye to them and walk out of their lives. They must be in so much pain already! I couldn't do that to them again. And I'm sure Soren probably has somebody watching the house. It would be suicide for me to try to see them. Even worse, I might be putting Momma, Papa, Julia, and Nicholas at risk if I try to contact them.

My foot presses on the accelerator and the Civic leaps forward, following the signs to London, Ontario and Detroit instead. It's only seven p.m. Eastern Time, but I've been travelling for eleven hours. I feel like I can drive for a couple of hours before I need to stop for some sleep. I slide in behind a tractor-trailer and turn on the radio for company.

The first station I find is an oldies station. That's okay. My mind is wandering and I'm not really listening to it anyway. The sun sinks lower in the sky. I notice some orange leaves starting to show on a few maple trees, reminding me that it will be September in a few days. If everything had gone according to my original plan, Julia and Nicholas would have been living with me and starting school in New York in a few days. This time as I remember the events in New York, instead of feeling sadness, I find myself starting to feel angry for the first time.

That fucking Soren. Why did he have to be such a phony! Why couldn't he just leave me alone? Why did I have to follow his money trail? Why couldn't I just turn a blind eye?

"Fucking asshole!" I scream. I realize I'm shouting at the top of my lungs to nobody in particular.

Okay, Angela. Take a deep breath and calm down.

I focus on my breathing as I watch the tail lights of the tractor-trailer in front of me. Before I know it, I'm humming along with the radio. I see more brown and orange leaves on the trees. New York City. Winter. I realize I'm humming along to

California Dreamin'. It's not the version I'm used to — this sounds like the Beach Boys. A winter's day. California. The seed of an idea starts forming in my head.

Why not California? Where else am I going to go? Warm winters. Sunshine. Yeah... why not?

My little Honda Civic rumbles louder as it climbs the long haul up the Niagara escarpment leading away from Toronto. It's getting dark and I turn on the headlights. My stomach gurgles. I realize I can't deny my body's urges much longer. I watch the highway signs. Guelph. Cambridge. Kitchener. London. It looks like there are plenty of choices for food and lodging ahead.

I find myself humming again. This time it's the mellow sound of Nat King Cole. I'm not much for listening to oldies, but Momma and Papa had Nat King Cole's greatest hits, and I grew up with his smooth, relaxing sound. *Get Your Kicks on Route 66*. My idea was starting to germinate.

Route 66. Why not?

They say the old highway's hardly there anymore. Only a few sections remain. I've seen photo essays that portray what still exists of the legendary old trail through the Midwest and southwest, from Chicago to Los Angeles. Even the photos of small town decay have a romantic quality to them. I drive onward, thinking of all the things to be seen between Chicago and California. The Grand

Canyon… I've always wanted to see it… Las Vegas… maybe not. Too many people and I might be recognized. I remind myself again that I'm on the run and I can't let anybody recognize me.

I make up my mind. Route 66 to Los Angeles it is. I'll stop and buy a Triple A membership when I get into Michigan. Who knows? The Civic might need some towing before I get there, and I can pick up some maps. I should also get myself a ball cap and some sunglasses. Maybe some hair dye. I need to start being careful about where I go and how I look. The stark reality of my situation hits me yet again. I've disconnected myself from the rest of the world.

I am completely alone.

CHAPTER 8

I HAVE a hard time believing that it's March, 2006, three years since that fateful day when Dori and I went to see Pastor Soren Kristiansen's ministry in Cleveland. If anybody had told me how that night would affect my life, I would gladly have stayed home. I would have kept myself from being lonely by continuing to reach out to other hopeful souls on the WWCC chat line. I wouldn't have attended the Ministry event that night. Twenty-twenty hindsight is wonderful, isn't it?

I look around me at the crowd of people sitting or lying on the grass in San Julian Park on this warm spring day. I'm trying to convince myself that hasn't been so bad living in Los Angeles for the past six months. I'm not the only person in the park with a history. Everybody else who lives on the street has their own story. But there's an unwritten code amongst the residents on the street — you don't ask anybody to talk about themselves. If they choose to share, you listen. If they don't talk, you don't ask.

I fall into the latter category. I nod respectfully to the people I see on a regular basis. They nod back in acknowledgement. Sometimes we make small talk about the weather, or about the Lakers or Dodgers. Other times, we might share whatever meagre food or drink we have in our possession that day. I know that some of the others are suspicious of me — I'm just as suspicious of them — but that's okay. We respect each other's paranoia. Now that spring is here and the weather is getting warmer, I've spent a few nights sleeping on the grass in the park. But over the winter, I always disappeared before nightfall, making sure that nobody followed me. I don't show up in the Skid Row neighborhood or the park every day. My routine is unpredictable. I like it that way.

I've made one exception for another regular visitor to San Julian. She calls herself Sally, but I know it's not her real name — just like she knows that Grace isn't mine. It's hard to tell how old Sally is. I'm guessing she's about five years older than my thirty-nine years, but Sally isn't wearing her years well. The remnants of red hair from her youth, now faded and hidden by layers of dull grey, give a hint of her youthful beauty from years gone by. Her freckled face is weathered and wrinkled, looking more like parchment than skin. I suspect that alcohol and drugs have played a large part in stealing her natural beauty and the sparkle from her eyes, judging from the small brown bag she carries each day.

"You don't have to name names, but who are you running from? The cops? A guy?" Sally asks.

"A little of both," I admit, fearing that even those four small words could be dangerous if spoken to the wrong person.

"What about you?" I answer.

"My boyfriend. He's one of the Angels. It was okay most of the time. He kept me safe for a lot of years," she says, little emotion in her voice.

"Did you love him?" I ask.

"Love?" Sally says, half laughing and half talking as she answers. "I'd say it was more like mutual respect. I let him fuck me whenever he wanted, and he kept me safe in return. I respected his right to fuck other women whenever he wanted, and he respected my right to shut-the-fuck-up. It worked. I couldn't complain."

Sally shrugs it off and reaches for her brown bag, pulling a small bottle of Canadian Club from its wrapper. She twists off the top, looks around for anybody in authority, takes a quick swig, then offers it to me.

"Want some?" she asks.

"Thanks, I'll pass," I say, a smile on my face. "I want to stay sober in case I have to run off to a business meeting."

We both burst out laughing.

"Good one," Sally says. She has no idea I'm not joking. I'm just laughing at the absurd duality of my secret life.

"Any kids?" Sally asks. I think I see her eyes getting a bit red and watery.

"Yeah. Two," I answer, feeling the sudden need to swallow a big lump that suddenly forms in my throat. "And you?"

"Four," Sally responds. "Three of them have left home, but my baby girl is just thirteen."

"So what happened?" I ask. "Something upset the mutual respect?"

"Yup. You could say that," she snorts. "Why else would I leave my kid? The pigs caught me runnin' some money for a big deal that was goin' down. I didn't tell them squat," she says bitterly, then tips back another huge swig of whiskey.

"They let you go?" I inquire.

"Sure, they let me go. They offered me witness protection to give evidence, but I didn't bite. They kept sayin' they weren't interested in me. I could save myself by sellin' out Tony and the others. They knew they didn't have anything on me. But they knew I was dead if they let me go. I knew I was dead either way," she says. "You sure you don't want a drink?"

I shake my head and Sally takes another hit of CC, letting out a grunt and opening her eyes wide as the harsh liquid hits her stomach. Licking her lips, she continues as if nothing just happened.

"So when I got home, I tried to tell Tony I didn't squeal, but he got all paranoid on me. He kept askin' me what they asked. He couldn't let it go. He wanted to know exactly what I said, word for word. He was wasted, and he started beatin' on me. He wouldn't stop. The other guys finally had to pull him off, cuz they were afraid he was goin' to kill me. They didn't give a shit about me. They were just worried about their own asses."

The alcohol is lowering Sally's filter. She isn't aware she's letting Tony's name slip. She tips the whiskey back again, and I'm shocked at how fast it's disappearing.

"It took a few days for me to get right. But nobody would talk to me. I knew Tony was done with me. He couldn't trust me anymore. I think he thought I was workin' with the pigs now. An' I knew what usually happens to people when Tony doesn't trust 'em. They just disappear."

"So you took matters into your own hands," I say.

"Yup, they were all partyin' at the club one Saturday night. I knew they'd all be wasted by mornin'. I found a pile of cash on Tony's desk. He got sloppy an' didn't put it in the safe yet. It was my ticket out an' I knew I had to take it. I might not get another chance. After that, there was no turnin' back. I told them I had a migraine an' had to go home. I took a cab out of town, an' jumped on the first Greyhound I could catch. I never got off till that bus reached the Pacific."

Sally almost drains her bottle with the next gulp of amber anesthetic.

"What about you, Gracie?" she asks.

I pause and choose my words carefully, grateful I hadn't accepted Sally's offer of a drink. My filters and defenses are still up. I can't afford to let them down.

"Let's just say I found some irregularities in my boss's company books," I hint. "When he found out I was onto him, he threatened to tell the cops that I was the brains behind the crime. Then he tried bullying me into joining him by saying it would be a shame if anything happened to my kids. I know a threat when I hear one."

I look at Sally. Her mind is seriously impaired, but I see the wheels still turning slowly.

"You couldn't just walk away. You had to steal some insurance, didn't you? Just like me." The hint of a twinkle glows briefly in Sally's eyes, and a wide grin spreads across her face. She salutes me with the nearly-empty bottle, before tipping it back and draining it.

"Ahhh… Good for you," she says. "Us girls, we gotta take care of ourselves." She leans forward and puts both arms around me. I accept her embrace, not realizing how much I've needed to feel a thread of connection to another human, no matter how slender that thread. I find myself clutching her body and patting her back. It feels so good to hold another person. My mind drifts and I wonder what it would be like to find comfort in each other's arms. For an instant, I have an image of Sally and me lying naked together, holding each other tight. I give my head a shake and bring myself back into the present, to Sally's last words.

"We do indeed, Sally. A girl's gotta do what a girl's gotta do, right?"

For just a moment, I see Sally's eyes starting to water. Then, with a huge sniffle, she sucks it up and re-employs her defenses. She pushes her shoulders back in a brave attempt to look strong again. We sit silently for a few seconds, looking into each other's eyes. At that moment, we both understand completely what the other is going through, and allow ourselves to feel mutual empathy.

"So, I'll see ya 'round?" Sally asks.

"Yeah, I'll see you around," I assure Sally. "Where else would I go? I like this park. I feel like it's a safe oasis. I can sit by this wall, feel the warmth of the sun, and nobody can sneak up behind me. It's the only time I feel like I can relax for an hour or two."

"I know what you mean. I like you, Gracie. I gotta go an' find me a place to piss now."

With that abrupt announcement, Sally rises to her feet with great effort, teetering precariously for an instant before her senses catch up and provide her with some balance. She gives me a silent wave and turns away, weaving her way unsteadily through the bodies that cover the tiny park's lawn, before crossing the street and disappearing around the corner.

I wonder what Sally would think if she knew that I actually have three different faces. There's the face of the missing Angela Baranyi, the face I have to keep hidden from the rest of the world. Then there's the face of down-on-her-luck Grace Wagner, the street person, that I allow the residents of San Julian Park to see. Finally, there's the face of Anna Benz. I wonder what Sally would say if she could see the small second-floor office that Anna Benz Developments has renovated on South Figueroa, about half way between San Julian and the main USC campus. I wonder if she would even recognize the impeccably-dressed, sharp businesswoman who is the new owner of a half dozen rundown student homes near the university.

Only when the business meetings are over, when Anna Benz peels away the veneer of success and transforms back into Angela Baranyi, when I replace my designer suits, blouses, and dresses with my dirty, torn, putrid-smelling blue jeans, threadbare t-shirt, sunglasses and hoodie, would Sally recognize me as Gracie Wagner.

I can only stay in San Julian Park for so long before I have to leave. The longer I stay, the more I find myself starting to sink into loneliness, sadness, and guilt. And before long, if I don't leave, I find myself drowning in depressive thoughts. Putting on the face of Anna Benz and retreating to her South Figueroa office is the only thing that keeps me sane.

I pull the peak of my ball cap down over my sunglasses and rise to my feet. I gather up my few belongings and stuff them into a plastic grocery bag. I drop the bag into the wire basket on the handlebars of a bicycle that leans up against the wall beside me. The bike is my best purchase so far. It takes forever to ride the bus the relatively short distance to my office, and people have nothing better to do than stare at other passengers. I can't afford to have somebody recognize me, and it only takes a few minutes to cover the same distance to the office by bicycle.

I walk the bike through the park to the street, look behind me for oncoming vehicles, and then I ride out onto West 5th street, heading towards Figueroa. I'm looking forward to a shower and spending the night on the pull-out bed in my office. Tomorrow, I put on the face of Anna Benz, real estate and property developer.

Unlike most days, I'm looking forward to tomorrow. I have a meeting scheduled with an ambitious young developer whom my new lawyer recommended. I have to keep telling myself to look at the bright side. It's another day of freedom from Soren Kristiansen. But other parts of my identity tell me it's also another day of living in loneliness. And another day of living in constant fear that somebody is going to find me.

IT TOOK me a few weeks to decide upon the best way to launder my ill-gotten fortune. I spent countless hours devising a complicated layering scheme, where I would spend a great deal of energy transferring random, small amounts of money between accounts to avoid raising the suspicions of Big Brother, who is always watching for just that kind of activity. Then, one day while I sat with my back against the wall in San Julian, soaking up some late autumn warmth, the solution to my problem suddenly dawned on me.

Occam's razor. Of course! The simplest solution is usually the best. Soren Kristiansen was laundering his money by investing in real estate in his church's name. Why can't I invest in real estate too? Then I realized that my solution was only about four miles away at USC — thousands of students from all over America and the world who need a place to live while they attend the prestigious university. Student housing: a lucrative market that never disappears.

T.J. Rhodes is the capable young contractor who did the renovations on my first venture, a rundown old home near the campus. My dilemma at that time was whether to bulldoze the place or try to renovate. Everybody I talked to was trying to get me to rebuild. But T.J. convinced me that it wouldn't pay to build a new building on such a small lot. I really needed to get at least two lots side by side to make a project worthwhile. Then, he explained, I could build an apartment block with multiple units to generate more income.

One year later, it's March 2006 and I realize now how lucky I was to find T.J. He's young and ambitious, hard-working, and he's a perfectionist like me. He's not content on just getting a project done as cheaply as possible, he wants to make sure people recognize his work and want to hire him for their next project. He's my kind of business person. So far, we've worked together on six projects.

He also spends his limited leisure hours in the gym, building a body with muscles that ripple under his tight t-shirts — definite eye candy for the women. But I haven't been able to figure out yet if he's got anybody in his life.

I'm sitting across the table from T.J., looking over the final draft of the architect's drawings. I'm feeling motivated and optimistic about this project. More importantly, I'm finally starting to believe in myself — to believe that I might actually be able to create a future for myself. I'm starting to have more positive days than those where I feel hopeless.

"These are great, Anna," T.J. says with enthusiasm. "I love the changes the architect has made. They make much better use of the space in these corner apartments, and it will make them easier and cheaper to construct. What do you think?"

"I agree," I reply. "I'm starting to think we've got something we can move forward with."

"I'm with you," he answers. "I'll get my lawyer to draw up a tentative contract so we're ready when we get some numbers. Can I go ahead and give this to my estimator?"

"I can't see any reason why not," I answer. "I'm really glad to be working with you on this, T.J. I appreciate your experience and your input with all the planning."

"Don't mention it," he says. "I've learned that the little bit of time I spend on this now, the more time and money we save when we actually put the shovels to the dirt. I appreciate how you're able to cut through the crap and get to the important issues. You have no idea how much time *that* saves. Where did you learn such good business sense?"

His question causes my body to stiffen.

Okay, this is uncomfortable. Let's talk about anything else besides me! Try to change the subject.

"From my dad," I lied. "I helped him with his books, so he showed me a lot about running a business. And I'm pretty good at seeing things from the bottom line, because I started off as an accountant. It's nothing, really. I just picked it up as I went along. So, when do you think you'll have the estimates ready?"

Okay, T.J. Enough about me. Please… let's talk about the estimates!

"You know, Anna. This is the seventh project we've done together, and I realize I don't really know much about you, except that it seems like we tend to see things the same way. What do you say about getting together for dinner some night? To discuss business."

Oh my God! Is he hitting on me? He must see that I'm not wearing a ring. This is the last thing I need.

"That's very kind of you," I answer, trying my hardest to keep the atmosphere professional. "But I really like to keep my business and personal lives separate. I hope you understand."

T.J pauses and takes a moment to look into my eyes. I hate being the center of attention and I start fidgeting. The silence seems like it's never-ending, until he finally breaks the awkward hush.

"There's something about you that's hard to resist, Anna. You're beautiful, and I see a woman who is extremely intelligent. But there's more than that. I think I see fear… maybe loneliness, in your eyes. I can't help but wonder what's made you that way."

I pause, searching for words. Anything to shut him down and to stop him from asking more questions about me.

"I'm a good ten years older than you, T.J. And you don't know anything at all about me," I say, almost begging him to stop now.

"I know, Anna. But think about it. You and I are a lot alike. I'm so busy with my work, I haven't been able to make any relationships last. I think you're the same. There's something that stops you from committing too, isn't there? We could be just right for each other — working together during the day, but there for each other at the end of the day?"

Okay, now I'm starting to feel really uncomfortable. How can he tell so much about me? This is getting too close for comfort. It feels dangerous… and it just feels wrong.

I start to feel panic taking hold of my body. My stomach is churning, my chest is tight and I'm having trouble breathing. I feel myself starting to tremble all over. I manage a weak smile.

"Tell you what, T.J., I'll think about it, okay?" I say, hoping to buy myself some time.

His face brightens and a sense of relief spreads across his face.

"Thanks," he answered. "If we're going to be working so closely, we might as well get to know each other better. Who knows where it could go, right?"

Nowhere good is where it's going to go.

"Thanks for being patient with me," I answer, doing my best to stay calm and to look sincere. "Now, where were we?"

IT'S THE FOLLOWING day, and I'm sitting in the Figueroa office, looking over the finances for Anna Benz Developments. My mind is still distracted after yesterday's conversation and proposition from T.J.. I'm having trouble concentrating, so I turn down the volume on the small secondhand portable TV I purchased to help me keep up on what's happening in the world. Okay, I admit it. I also sit and watch an occasional sitcom to lighten my mood.

As I point the remote at the TV, an image on the screen leaps out at me. I feel the world start to spin. My entire body trembles and then freezes. I can't move my arms or legs. My chest suddenly feels like someone is sitting on it and I'm struggling to suck any air into my lungs. It's no wonder I'm having difficulty concentrating. I find myself staring into the eyes of Pastor Soren Kristiansen of the *World-Wide Community of Christ*, and I hear his voice as he's interviewed by KABC news. My eyes are so wide open that they almost pop out of my head as the reality starts to sink in.

Oh my God! He's in L.A. right now!

I feel myself breaking into a cold sweat, and I'm aware that I need to get some control over my panic. Easier said than done. I try to focus on slowing my breathing, but my eyes are riveted to the TV. Soren is talking about his ministry, which he's bringing to the Staples Center for two nights. I start feeling anger rising from deep inside my core. It gets in the way of being able to slow my breathing.

You hypocrite! You and I both know how fake that smile of yours is! And your messages of hope and love — what a bunch of bull! You ruined my life. When I was at my lowest, I put my faith in you and God and your messages. And you betrayed that faith. How can God let you get away with that?

It dawns on me that my fear of Soren is now overshadowed by my anger. I still feel tight, but I'm trembling as much from rage as from fear. I don't know what to do with my anger. I manage to raise my arm and point the remote at the TV. The room goes silent. I can't get the image of Soren, and the conflicting emotions of fear and rage, out of my mind. I'm terrified that he'll find out I'm in L.A.

But at the same time, I also feel like I want to reach out and strangle him!

I sit down at my desk and try to focus on finances again. The silence is helpful, but my mind keeps drifting off — trying to find a way to resolve the emotional conflicts in my mind. I keep bringing myself back to the financial ledger in front of me. The black and white numbers on the page have a way of grounding me, until I finally find myself lost in them. After about thirty minutes, I'm feeling satisfied that my decision to get into real estate is starting to pay off. I've only had to use about half of Soren's money to buy the first six properties, borrowing the rest to make the investments look more legitimate.

My cash flow is impressive, and I realize my developments are starting to become too much for me to manage on my own. I decide I can't keep doing my own books, and I need to hire a legitimate accountant, and probably a tax lawyer. I'm starting to believe that I can take care of myself for the rest of my life. Then, without warning, I find myself thinking of Soren again. I take a breath, sigh, then I say a small prayer to myself.

Dear God. I'm sorry for being so bitter towards You. I was wrong to be angry at You. I need to thank You for the good things that have come my way from Pastor Soren. Please help me find a way to put this money to good use for Julia and Nicholas. And

*please find a way to keep them safe from harm.
Amen. Angela.*

I think that reconnecting with God might help me feel better. But my feelings of thankfulness and optimism are still weighed down by fear, anger, and the overpowering feelings of guilt and loneliness over not being there for Julia and Nicholas, or for Momma and Papa.

It's clear now that yesterday's conversation with T.J., followed by seeing and hearing Soren on TV, has created a whirlwind of emotions inside me.

I know I shouldn't feel afraid, since everything has been going so well lately. I have limited dealings with people, and those who have seen my face haven't recognized me. And even though Soren will be in Los Angeles for the next two days, I know the chances of him seeing me are next to nothing. So why can't I can't seem to shake the feeling that something bad is going to happen — something that will disturb the safety and seclusion of my small, organized little world?

I decide it's time to go back to Skid Row for two or three days to simplify my life and get away from it all. I'll have a good sleep tonight, and I'll ride my bike back to San Julian Park tomorrow. I look forward to talking with Sally again. But just then, the seed of another idea starts to germinate in my mind. I may have just stumbled on a way to resolve some of my inner emotional conflicts. I realize there's one thing I must do before I go back underground.

CHAPTER 9

I FEEL MYSELF perspiring heavily in the March sunshine, not so much from the sun, as from my nerves. I'm blending in well with the crowd of thirty or forty people, mostly women, gathered outside the lobby of the Four Seasons hotel in Beverly Hills. I'm dressed in running tights, a long-sleeved running shirt, sneakers, and a running cap. I'm hoping, but I'm not totally confident, that my sunglasses and cap will cover most of my face.

The women in the crowd are all intent on only one thing — catching a glimpse, and maybe an autograph or a picture of their idol, Pastor Soren Kristiansen. They're being held at bay, across the pavement from the hotel entrance, by an overweight hotel security employee who can't be more than twenty, judging from the crop of pimples on his young face. He's sweating profusely under the arms of his brilliant white uniform shirt, partially from having to stand out in the midday sun, and partially because his plump body is struggling to cool itself. I laugh to myself, realizing how impotent he would be to stop this mob of screaming women from swarming Pastor Soren if that should happen.

The sweat on my hand makes it difficult to hold the video camera I'd brought with me. I dry my left hand on my tights, then transfer the camera to my left hand while I dry my right hand. For the fifth or sixth time, I make sure the camera is turned on, ready to start filming. I know I probably only have one chance to get this right and I don't want to screw it up.

"There he is!" shouts one of the women in the mob. My ears are pierced by a chorus of shrieks and screams. The sea of humanity flows around the useless security guard, as if he was invisible. My feet are frozen to the pavement, my heart racing and my arms shaking uncontrollably. Unlike the rest of the crowd, I can't risk getting too close to Soren. I feel panic rising in my body because I can't see over the rest of the women. Quickly, I look around and see a planter behind me. I hop up onto the retaining wall, giving myself a two-foot advantage.

And then I see him, still wearing his charming smile, just like a chameleon — making himself appear to be exactly what his fans want him to be — enigmatic and sexy. Remembering the video camera in my sweaty hand, I raise it to my face and look through the viewfinder. I press the *Start* button on the camera, and a red *Record* light appears in the finder. I realize I've been holding my breath, so I allow myself to exhale slowly, trying to steady the shaky image in the viewing screen.

My finger slides to the *Zoom* button and I press it, only to have the scene become smaller instead. I press the other side of the button and the scene grows larger, until Soren's head fills the center of the screen. He is in his glory, smiling at each woman as he signs autographs. I feel my body starting to relax, and I feel my confidence growing. I press the pause button and hop down off the retaining wall. I venture onto the pavement, crossing the road until I'm standing on the edge of the screaming swarm.

I flip out the camera's LCD screen, refocus the camera, start it recording again, and raise it high over my head. I'm almost starting to feel a bit cocky now. I'm shooting semi-blind from this close distance. Suddenly, a woman wraps her arm around Soren, and he complies by draping his arm around her shoulder as she poses for a picture. The woman's friend remains in the crowd, which automatically parts like the Red Sea to give her a clear path for her photo-op. I'm standing behind the photographer, with almost a clear path between myself and Soren. As he beams his insincere smile at the camera, I see his eyes move slightly until they're focused on me.

My body freezes instinctively, and I pray that my cap and sunglasses are doing their job. I see Soren's eyes squint and his forehead furrows. The smile disappears from his face and time feels like it's standing still for me. I feel his eyes wander over me, and I feel violated. I see and feel flashbacks of the times he touched me during our business meetings, almost feeling like it's happening again. I catch myself holding my breath, and I force myself to try breathing and acting normally. The fearful part of me is tempted to look away — to do anything to avoid eye contact with the man who surely wants to have me killed. But the angry part of me won't let me take my eyes off of Soren, and I continue to glare back at him. Fortunately, my sunglasses are shielding my stare from his prying eyes, and he can't see the loathing in them.

That's it, Soren. Look at me! I'm the one who took your dirty money. I'm the one who can bring you down whenever I choose.

Then, just as quickly, Soren's eyes leave me and return to the adoring fan beside him. He teases her with a kiss on the cheek and the remainder of the crowd screams with delight. The path between me and Soren fills again with bodies that flood into the empty space. Within seconds, I'm hidden from Soren's view by a sea of arms, all waving and reaching out with photos or pieces of paper in hopes of getting an elusive autograph.

Satisfied that I've captured more than enough video footage, I turn and walk away from the crowd. I head back towards South Doheny where I'd parked my bike. I'm tempted to run, but I resist the urge, not wanting to draw any attention to myself. I deftly open the camera bag that sits in the wire basket on the bike's handlebar. I slip the video camera back into the bag and zip it closed in one smooth motion. Donning my bike helmet over my running cap, I walk the bike back onto the street at a brisk pace, mount it, and disappear into traffic.

As the Four Seasons disappears behind me, I feel my chest release. My breathing starts to find a rhythm, synchronizing with the pumping of my legs. I feel self-confidence creeping back into my body. It's a feeling I haven't felt since the day I set Soren up for my disappearance. I allow myself to crack a small smile, before I feel the ever-present weight of loneliness and guilt settle on my shoulders again.

Despite the success of my mission today, I feel the familiar sense of foreboding creeping up on me. It's been following me like a shadow for the past two days, and I can't seem to shake it. I know today's successful mission is small consolation. But at least I feel an ounce of contentment, knowing that I now have even more insurance for dealing with Soren, just in case I ever need it.

IT'S LATE afternoon by the time I return to the office on Figueroa. I drop the camera bag on the table and flop down on my couch, feeling a flood of relief to be back in the one place in my world where I feel safe. I know it's time to change into my street clothes, and to disappear back into the underbelly of Los Angeles for a few days. I remember I have to change the message on my phone so T.J. and my small circle of business contacts know I'm away for a few days. Wearily, I find the remote for the TV and turn it on to break the silence.

I rummage through my small bar fridge for something to eat, knowing that my meals will be meagre for the next few days. Noticing some fruit and sandwich meat that needs to be used, I remove them and set them on the wooden cutting board, on top of the fridge, that doubles as a countertop. The TV drones on in the background while my ham and cheese sandwich takes shape. Suddenly the monotony of daytime programming is broken by an authoritative male voice from the local KCBS newsroom.

"… We have word of breaking news from our CBS affiliate in Palm Springs. For more on this story, we have Jenifer Daniels reporting."

"I'm live here in Palm Desert at the home of a well-known Los Angeles and Parisian art dealer, where police say two people have died. One of the victims appears to have drowned, while the other died of gunshots wounds on the way to Eisenhower Hospital. Details are still sketchy…"

My curiosity gets the best of me, so I drift over to the couch and sit down with my sandwich while I watch the news.

"… Unconfirmed reports have suggested that these two deaths may be related in some way to the recent disappearance of a Columbian couple from LAX about one month ago…"

Suddenly my jaw locks in mid-bite, as I gaze past the blonde news reporter, to the wall behind her. I'm stunned to find myself staring at an enormous black-and-white photograph of myself, hanging on the wall of the estate behind the reporter.

I'm horribly confused, and none of this makes sense until I gaze once again into the eyes of my likeness. I recognize fear and distrust in my eyes. And in that instant, I know immediately when the picture was taken.

"… This is Jenifer Daniels, reporting from Palm Desert."

I barely hear the words of the reporter as she signs off. My mind flashes back to that afternoon in San Julian Park last fall. I remember the feeling of dread as the woman with short black hair and her old SLR camera walked into the park, focusing both her attention and the camera on me. I should have leapt to my feet and bolted from the park. But for the first time, I now realize that I was just as captivated by the woman behind the camera, as she was by me. But I also realize that my curiosity and my failure to run could potentially cost me my life.

Stupid! How could you have been so stupid? What if Soren sees that picture? He'll know somebody's seen me and he'll start digging. What if Momma and Papa see it? Or Julia and Nicholas? What will they think of me?

All of a sudden, even San Julian Park and Skid Row don't feel safe anymore.

If Soren finds out who took that picture, he'll know where it was taken!

I feel my mind accelerating into panic mode. I've spent many hours sitting by myself, surrounded by the other street people in east downtown Los Angeles, casually thinking about what I'd do if this day ever came. Now it's here, and my mind is blank. I'm only certain of one thing. It's too dangerous to stay in Los Angeles.

Where else am I going to live? What am I going to do about my business and my properties? What am I going to say to T.J.?

My old friend fear has returned with a vengeance. And along with it, so does anger, loneliness, and guilt that start building inside me. I feel angry at myself for getting involved with Soren in the first place. And I feel a deep resentment that I now have to spend my life running and hiding from him. Then there's the almost overpowering loneliness and guilt over being apart from Julia and Nicholas.

Before I know it, the dam has burst and I find myself weeping inconsolably. I feel completely overwhelmed. I don't know if I have the energy to keep doing this. I feel myself sinking into a bottomless pit of hopelessness and despair. The tears continue to rain from my eyes. For the first time in my life, I start thinking how easy it would be if I just wasn't here anymore. At least then there would be a corpse and my family wouldn't have to wonder what happened to me anymore.

I start seeing images of how it might end for me. I start wondering if the light fixture in the ceiling is strong enough to hold my weight for a few minutes until it's all over. Then I see myself just walking into the Pacific, swimming out into the currents and letting them carry me away.

I become vaguely aware of a sensation gnawing in the pit of my stomach, barely discernible against the overwhelming blackness of my despair. The gnawing sensation starts to grow, making me feel nauseous. My body tenses again, especially my fists. I start recognizing the sensation. It's my other old friend, anger.

Angela, listen to me! You're not going to let Kristiansen win, are you? You're stronger than that! Pull yourself together, girl. Look at what you've accomplished over the past six months as Anna

Benz! Someday you'll find a way to get your old life back. You can do it. You cannot let that bastard win!

My sobbing gradually ebbs to a slow series of sniffles. My body is still trembling, but I feel myself rising towards the surface of the bottomless pool of despair. The image of that portrait is now burned into my memory. I close my eyes and focus on my likeness from the photograph. I'm staring into my own eyes again — Angela's eyes — the Angela from San Julian Park.

I see a woman who is strong — a woman who trusts her instincts and is true to herself, instead of letting herself be controlled, manipulated, and abused by a man like Soren Kristiansen. I start feeling a sense of pride in that woman, and I imagine that she's talking to me.

You did it once, and you can do it again, Angela. You owe it to yourself and your children!

And then I remember my friend Sally from San Julian — how she's given up on herself, and how she only has her next bottle of Canadian Club to look forward to.

I open my eyes and re-orient myself back into my South Figueroa office — back into the land of the living. My body is still trembling. I realize I'm still afraid. But I realize I'm no longer afraid of Soren Kristiansen. I'm afraid of how close I just came to ending my own life. And after looking into my own eyes, I vow that I'm never going back to that place again.

I GUIDE MY trusty Honda Civic down East Flamingo in Las Vegas, looking for the address of the two-story strip mall in the advertisement. I'm only a few minutes east of The Strip, but the landscape has changed drastically as I drive east. I see the address I'm looking for, and I pull the Civic into the parking lot.

The building doesn't look old. I remind myself that most of this city is relatively new, having sprung up out of the desert over the past forty years. Instead, the word *tired* comes to mind as I survey the building. The stucco exterior is grimy from years of desert dust settling into its pores. White paint peels from the iron railing on the second floor, the onset of rust providing evidence of the occasional rains that pour down on the area, leaving a trail of flash floods before sunshine and bone-dry air return.

My mind drifts to the large vacant areas of land in this sprawling city, each one with black tunnels exiting from underground floodways that sprawl unseen beneath the opulence and neon of the city. The floodways and emergency reservoirs act as a reminder of the frailty of life in the desert, where rain can bring both life and death at the same time.

They remind me of how fragile and vulnerable my life is right now — how being seen by the wrong person at the wrong moment in time can mean sudden danger, and possibly death, for me.

A silver Mercedes driven by an Asian man pulls up beside me in parking lot, bringing me out of my daydream. I climb out of the Civic and extend my hand to greet the building's owner.

"Hello, I'm Anna Benz," I say. "Thank you for meeting me, Mr. Lau."

"You are most welcome," he says, speaking in very precise English that reveals an educated background. "Follow me, and I will show you the space."

I climb the metal stairs on the building's exterior, following Mr. Lau to the second floor landing. When I reach the top, I stop and look westward, where the Spring and Nopah mountain ranges shimmer against a brilliant blue sky on this calm spring day. I hear the key in the lock and Mr. Lau opens the door to the vacant office space.

As I walk into the space, the air smells old and stagnant. It's already becoming very hot inside; it's clear that the space has been empty for a while, with no air conditioning to move the air. The skittering sound of a telltale cockroach tells me that a good cleaning and extermination are in order. The neutral-colored walls are dirty and grey, and the cheap office-grade carpet is flattened and worn.

Looking up to the roof, I see yellow stains, left behind by a leaky roof or air conditioning unit.

"I see there's been some leaks from the roof," I observe. "When did that happen?"

"Two or three years ago," he says. "The air conditioning unit was not draining properly, but it is fixed now. There is no more leak."

"How much?" I ask.

"One thousand dollar per month. Five-year lease," Mr. Lau replies.

"No lease, month to month," I say without a pause. "I'll pay you eight-fifty per month, cash in advance for six months." I see Mr. Lau quickly doing the math in his head, trying to figure out how he can save with this cash deal.

"Nine hundred and you have a deal, Ms. Benz," he says politely.

"Okay, I'll take it. I'll pay one month today, and the other five months next week, when I move in." I reach into my pocket and pull out a wad of hundred dollar bills, counting ten and handing them to Mr. Lau. "Here's my phone number. Call me first, and I can meet you at your convenience to pick up the keys and pay the balance."

"What kind of business are you in?" Mr. Lau asks, his eyes narrow and his voice full of suspicion.

"I'm in property development and management," I say, my voice strictly businesslike.

I feel the back of my neck bristling. My guard goes up automatically, as it does whenever anybody starts asking me questions about myself.

"I've been working in Los Angeles, and I want to expand to Las Vegas. My partner will be handling the Los Angeles office while I work here," I say, giving him the bare minimum of information to answer his question.

"I wish you good fortune," Mr. Lau says, bowing slightly. The crease in his forehead, along with the suddenly cool look in his eyes, signals a disparity between his verbal message and his real feelings. Mr. Lau clearly isn't happy to have another competitor in town.

"Thank you, Mr. Lau," I reply politely, painting a smile on my face. The last thing I need is to make an enemy in my new home city. "You've been most kind to show me the space on such short notice."

Mr. Lau follows me along the landing and down the stairs. We shake hands one more time, and then I climb back into the Civic, which has transformed into a sauna while I've been in the building. I press the button to lower the windows, allowing some of the stifling heat to escape. I feel a fleeting sense of relief wash over me as I guide the small vehicle back onto Tropicana, heading towards I-15. I know I have a new base for my life. Moving out of Los Angeles can't happen soon enough.

But as I think of Los Angeles, my chest suddenly becomes tight and I feel that dreaded weight descending on it again. My heart is pounding and my breathing is short and rapid. I'm having a panic attack and realize I need to get off the road. I swing into a left turn lane and race to catch a green arrow, which turns yellow just as I reach the intersection. My foot pounds on the accelerator and the Civic's engine roars to life. The tires squeal and I feel my body being dragged to the right by the force of my turn.

I find myself in a parking lot and I pull into the first open space I find. Instinctively, I close my eyes and start talking myself through the routine I've come to know so well.

You can do this, Angela. Slow down your breathing. Don't try to breathe too deeply — nice smooth breaths — just feel the air flowing into your lungs — feel it flowing out — feel the tension releasing from your muscles…

Gradually, I feel the tension draining from my body. My heart gradually slows and my breathing stabilizes.

What brought that on? What made you feel so anxious? What were you thinking when it started?

I try to reconnect with my thoughts after I left Mr. Lau at the office space.

The I-15 sign for Los Angeles. That's it! You don't want to go back. You can't go back there. But what are you going to do for a week until you meet Mr. Lau? Where are you going to live?

My mind goes into problem-solving mode, oblivious to everything going on around me at the moment.

Go back to L.A. one more time, Angela — just to clean out the Figueroa office. See if T.J. can help. You can rent a U-Haul in Vegas, drive to L.A. to pack up your things, and get back here in a day. You'll just need to find a safe place to stay for a week.

I find myself staring at the Tropicana Hotel and casino, whose parking lot I turned into when my panic attack overwhelmed me. An image flashes into my mind from earlier in the day, while I was driving north on Las Vegas Boulevard, just south of Tropicana. The image forms the seed of an idea, which gradually starts to germinate and to link with recollections of recent magazine articles and videos I've seen of Las Vegas.

A good sporting goods store. You need good camping gear — sleeping bag, flashlights or a headlamp, batteries — the bare minimum, so you can travel light.

I put my mind into *Rewind*, trying to remember all of the places I'd seen while driving around Las Vegas in my search for office space. Everything is a blur. My bare-bones cell phone has no internet access, so I decide to go into the Tropicana to find a phone book with Yellow Pages. I climb out of the Civic and lock the door, my mind now engrossed in the survival plan that is growing and becoming more clear with each passing moment. I feel myself starting to smile, feeling a weight lifting off my chest and shoulders. I find myself looking forward to the safety of the Las Vegas version of San Julian Park.

T.J. ROLLS the dolly with my bar fridge up the ramp into the U-Haul cube-van and maneuvers it into place. After he extracts the dolly, he leans on the device and looks down at me from the truck.

"That's it," he says. "Are you sure this is what you really want to do, Anna?"

"Yeah, T.J., I'm sure. Los Angeles is too big for me. I'll only be a few hours away in Vegas, and I'm sure you can handle most of the routine stuff with the local properties."

I smile up at my new business partner. T.J. was flattered when I'd asked if he wanted to be more than just a contractor — if he wanted to be my partner in property development and management. I made him an offer that he couldn't refuse. But he was definitely shocked by my next announcement — that I wanted to move to Las Vegas.

"Besides, the real estate market in Vegas is booming," I argued. "Now that prices around L.A.

are out of this world, a lot of people see having a home in Nevada as a viable option. I want to get in on that action. Besides, I like the lifestyle in Vegas. Once you get away from the strip, it's not crowded and it's easier to get around than Los Angeles."

T.J. fastens the dolly inside the back of the U-Haul and walks down the ramp. We pick up the ramp and push it back into the truck, locking it securely in place. Satisfied that all of my belonging are aboard, I turn to T.J.

"I can't thank you enough, T.J. We'll be talking every Monday morning at eight, and you can always call my cell phone and leave a message. Once we get the apartment building under construction, I'll come into L.A. every now and then to see how things are going. We'll have to meet once in a while with the lawyer and accountant anyways."

"I know," T.J. says. "This isn't goodbye. I appreciate everything you've done for me, Anna. Make sure you find us some good opportunities in Vegas, and then I'll have a reason to come and visit you."

"I'll look forward to that," I say, realizing I mean what I've just said. I've grown to trust and like T.J. a lot over the past six months. He's starting to feel just as much a friend, as a business partner. But I'm also aware that T.J. sees me as being more than a friend or business partner. It makes me feel sad that I don't feel the same physical attraction for him.

"I've got to go," I say. "I still have to get this truck unloaded and return it tonight."

I shake T.J.'s hand, then there's an awkward pause. We embrace each other and he gives me a farewell kiss on my cheek. I climb into the truck, feeling tiny in the large cab rather than the cozy confines of my Civic. As the truck's engine roars to life, and I pull away from the Figueroa office for the last time, an uneasy feeling starts descending on me.

I'm confused because I know I should be feeling a sense of relief. But, at the same time that I'm starting to feel safer by moving to Las Vegas, I still feel the same sense of foreboding that I felt before I saw my portrait on the TV news. And for the life of me, I can't figure out why I feel this way.

Maybe it's because deep down inside, I'm beginning to realize that living the rest of my life 'just being safe' may not be any kind of a life at all.

CHAPTER 10

THE BEAM from my headlamp slices through an almost impenetrable darkness that does its best to swallow any invading light. I walk my trusty bicycle into the tunnel, which is about eight feet wide, but only six feet high. The ankle-high rubber boots on my feet splash through puddles and tiny streams of water as I venture into the darkness, part of the Las Vegas flood management system. The entrance is slippery from algae and moss and the air is dank and clammy. In the wire basket, hanging from the handlebars of the bike, I have a plastic shopping bag filled with enough food and water for a couple of days.

The floodway is only a ten-minute bicycle ride down Tropicana from my new office. Its entrance lies in a wash, just south of the Tropicana Hotel and Casino, with a view of the *Welcome to Las Vegas* sign on Las Vegas Boulevard to the south, and McCarran Airport to the southeast.

Over the past two weeks, the floodway has become my home in Las Vegas. This is where I pass away the daytime hours, waiting for darkness to descend, and for the glittering neon lights of the famous Las Vegas Strip to illuminate the night sky to the north. When I emerge into darkness after sunset, I walk or run my bicycle away from the tunnel as fast as I can, feeling like I need to avoid the Luxor's constantly moving searchlight, just across the street and to the south. I'm not sure which feels creepier, the incredible inky blackness of the tunnel, or the Luxor's searchlight when I emerge at the end of the day. Logically, I know the light searches the sky randomly and it's not searching for me, but my paranoia won't believe it.

I hear my feet sloshing along through the puddles and streams, while my headlamp and my eyes scour the darkness for my little camp. I feel a crunch under my left foot and freeze, wondering what I stepped on. My head looks down at my foot and the beam from my headlamp follows. A dead crayfish, looking pale in the bright light, lays lifeless and deformed in a puddle, looking small and insignificant in the vast emptiness of the tunnel. I feel an empathic connection with the creature at that moment. I imagine it feeling alone, small, and insignificant just before it was squashed by a force much bigger than itself — much like I feel about myself at this moment.

The sound of chirping crickets reverberates through the darkness, and it brings my mind back into the present. I resume walking my bike through the inky blackness until I've gone about two hundred yards, when a ghostly orange apparition emerges from the blackness. An orange tarp, hanging from metal hooks in the concrete ceiling, is the first of three that forms a flimsy wall around my bed. I use the words 'my bed' loosely. I stumbled upon the remnants of this small camp, which had clearly been abandoned for some time, when I finally summoned the nerve to explore the tunnels. I still marvel at the ingenuity of its creator, who had suspended the metal bed frame with wire from a metal grate and a manhole cover in the roof of the tunnel, then fitted a wooden door and a mattress onto the frame. My bed is safely suspended three feet above the tunnel's floor, immune from the dangerous flash floods that can sweep through the floodways with no warning whatsoever.

A person never knows when those torrents of water will come. A sudden thunderstorm fifteen or twenty miles away in the mountains can cause flash floods that take hours to reach Las Vegas. Without the maze of tunnels, the city would be at the mercy of those unexpected floods. And without the floodways, many of the homeless population of Las Vegas would have no place to go.

I lean my bicycle against a grocery cart that is parked against the concrete wall, abandoned by the previous tenant. I'm thankful I had it when I first moved my meagre supplies into the camp. I remove the shopping bag from the bike's basket and place it on a makeshift shelf, suspended by ropes from the rungs of a metal ladder that descends from the manhole cover above. Then I take a bottle of water, a couple of granola bars, a banana and an apple out of the bag, placing them on the blanket that covers the old mattress. As I pick up the bag to set it on the shelf, I realize I forgot something. I reach back into the bag and grab my can of bear spray. Feeling more safe, I hop up onto the bed and flick off the power switch of my headlamp.

Darkness swallows me instantly. I can't even see my hand in front of my face. Apart from the constant din of chirping crickets, I'm completely alone. Sitting in the darkness and near silence, I finally feel some semblance of security. My thoughts start to wander aimlessly.

I'm still conflicted about being in Vegas. On one hand, it's easy to get lost in the sea of humanity that marches up and down Las Vegas Boulevard, filling the casinos, and spilling out of a seemingly endless variety of shows. On the other hand, I know that the chances of running into somebody I know are pretty good. Almost everybody makes it to Las Vegas at some point in their lives. Meeting somebody I know is a chance that I just can't afford to take, so I avoid Las Vegas Boulevard, with its horde of tourists, as if it was the plague. I hide in my floodway home during the day, then I pedal my bike east on Tropicana to my office, as quickly as possible at the end of the day, taking furtive glances over my shoulder at the Luxor searchlight as I ride.

There is almost nothing to occupy myself in my refuge, apart from listening to music on my new iPod, trying to read paperback books by headlamp, sleeping, or getting lost in thought. I spend far too much time inside my own head, trying to figure out what I'm going to do with my future. I know I should push Anna Benz to start scouring the neighborhoods around UNLV for potential investment properties, but I haven't been able to force myself to go out in public during the day since I arrived two weeks ago.

My mind drifts and connects, yet again, to the event that sent shockwaves through my body and caused me to flee Los Angeles three weeks ago — seeing my own photograph in the background of that CBS News bulletin from Palm Springs. Somehow, I knew those candid photographs would come back to haunt me. I didn't know when or how, but I knew the day would come. I knew I couldn't risk having anybody seeing them. As far as the rest of the world had been concerned for the past eighteen months, Angela Baranyi was dead. I walked away from everything — my two kids, my parents — and I *ran* away from my job. As far as anybody was concerned, I had disappeared from the face of the earth.

And yet, seeing my face in the background of the news report wasn't a total shock. I recognized the look of fear and distrust that I was feeling at the time, when I looked into my eyes in the candid portrait. The same feelings swept through my body as I realized the implications of having my likeness displayed for all to see. With one quick glimpse of myself on TV, my entire world has been turned upside down.

Since that day three weeks ago, my mind has been spinning — continually replaying the events from eighteen months earlier. Could I have done anything differently? How did I, Angela Baranyi, the innocent, religious, hard-working single mother of two, ever manage to get involved in Soren Kristiansen's web of dishonesty, deceit, and crime? How did I become a criminal myself? No matter how many times I analyze the events in my mind, I haven't come up with answers to those questions. So the events keep replaying in my memory, like a motion picture that never ends.

With every passing day, I'm growing more and more dissatisfied and frustrated with running, hiding, and not being able to live my life as Angela Baranyi. But I'm also acutely aware that I'm becoming more paranoid each day, unable to stop its malignant growth. I'm stuck — unable to find the motivation to do anything except hide in the darkness when the sun shines, and then go to the seclusion of my office. There, I'm able to connect with the world via my computer each night after sunset. Then I give myself a sponge bath in the office's tiny bathroom and try to get some sleep, usually with little success. I feel myself sinking into depression, much like I did after I left David in Cleveland, and like when I first settled in Los Angeles eighteen months ago.

SUDDENLY, out of the darkness and rising over the sound of the crickets, I hear a distant splash. My body freezes and I reach for my bear spray. I see a flashlight wobbling its way through the dark, and the sound of footsteps grows louder.

"Who's there!" I shout.

The light jerks towards me, and I'm suddenly blinded by the unwelcome intrusion into my dark world. Instinctively, my hands go up in front of my face to protect both my eyes and my identity.

"Who are you?" says a husky voice that is also distinctively female. All I can see of the woman is an ominous dark silhouette, looming from behind the harsh illumination of her flashlight. "I'm not going to hurt you. I'm a journalist. I stumbled onto these tunnels a couple of months ago and realized that people like you are actually living here. I'm following up on a short article I did, hoping to turn the story into a book. Do you mind if I talk to you?"

What am I going to say? If I say no, she might be suspicious. Even worse, she might report me. If I say yes, she might expose my identity and I'll have to run again!

My body is gripped with fear. I feel myself trembling. My mouth opens and I realize words are coming out. I listen to myself, as though I'm observing me from the outside.

"Okay. But no pictures, and no names. You can't describe what I look like to anybody or I won't talk. Agreed?"

"Sure," she says. "I'm okay with that. I always protect my sources. You're scared, is that why you're down here?"

I pause, wondering how much to say.

"Yeeeeeah," I mumble. "Let's just say I'm taking some time to be alone… to figure some things out."

Silence hangs in the air after my last words. All I can hear is the sound of my breathing and the distant sound of chirping crickets in the darkness. "Are you still there?" I ask.

"Your voice sounds familiar… that accent. Do I know you?"

My body goes rigid. My protective walls go up. I lower my right hand and it moves slowly until it feels the can of bear spray. My grip tightens, ready to aim the nozzle in the direction of the voice and the bright light in front of me. At the same time, my brain reaches the same conclusion. Where have I heard that husky feminine voice before?

"I don't think so," I answer, desperately wanting to change the subject. "Do you mind taking that light off me? Maybe shine it at the ceiling or something?"

"I'm sorry. Sure. Mind if I set it on your shelf over there?"

I nod and the woman points her light upward so that it reflects off the low ceiling and illuminates my entire camp with a dim yellow glow. My eyes are still adjusting to the light. But, for the first time, I'm able to see the woman as something other than a silhouette. She's medium height and dressed in army fatigues that emphasize her stocky frame. She has short, spiked, blonde hair. Even in the dim light, I can see her piercing blue eyes. On her right hip, I see a holster attached to her belt with some kind of a weapon. The pockets of her fatigues are bulging with equipment. A DSLR camera is suspended from a strap over her right shoulder.

"Okay, lady with no name, I'm Ricki… Ricki Marshall. How did you find out about the tunnels and how long have you been living here?" she asks.

I start laughing out loud at the coincidence. I realize that Ricki still hasn't recognized me, probably because of my disheveled appearance. My stringy, matted hair hangs partially over my face.

"I saw your article about the floodway online a couple of weeks ago when I first came to Vegas. That's how I found out about them. Do you suppose there's going to be a whole migration of people like me moving down here to escape from reality after they read your article?"

Ricki laughs at my joke, helping to put me a bit more at ease.

"I guess we'll see how many people I run into," she says. "Is that what you're doing? Escaping? Tell you what — I promise that I'll only write that you ran away from some overwhelming stress in your life. I'll keep the details of your story off the record if you'll talk with me."

I find myself feeling more at ease with Ricki, now that I know who she is. I sense the same genuine concern in her voice that I felt when I first met her in New York. How long ago was that? Has it really been almost two years?

"Weren't *you* afraid to come down here alone?" I ask timidly. I see Ricki eyeing me carefully. She's still trying to figure out how she knows me.

"Naw. I've never been one to be afraid, even when I probably should be. Don't worry, I've got my Taser, my bear spray, and a collapsible club within reach. Nobody wants to tangle with me."

"I don't doubt it for a minute," I say, chuckling.

"Did you build all of this yourself?" Ricki asks. "I'm impressed at your resourcefulness if you did."

"Sorry to disappoint," I concede. "I'm afraid I inherited it from someone who came before me." I feel my defensive walls starting to come down slowly. I realize that it feels good to be having some human contact.

"You wanted to know why I came down here?" I ask.

"Oh, yeah. What are you trying to figure out?" Ricki asks.

I pause, considering how much to tell her. I hear water trickling, the distant chirping of crickets.

"Whether I can keep running and hiding. Whether I can keep living with the guilt, I suppose."

"Guilt?" Ricki asks. "You left somebody behind? Husband, kids, lover?"

"I'd rather not say," I answer, trying to keep my cards close to my chest. But I realize that my non-answer told her what she wanted to know.

"Okay, I think I get it," Ricki says. She's staring at me again. She knows that she's seen me somewhere before, but she's still trying to put the pieces together. "Do you have any other options?"

"Yeah," I say, nodding. "I've created another identity. I could live another life. I might even learn to be happy. Or I can keep running."

"But either way, you're still hiding, aren't you?" Ricki asks rhetorically.

I don't answer right away, only nodding my
head up and down.

"You must have walked away from something
pretty important," she adds.

I nod my head up and down again.

"I'm getting the feeling that you don't think the
running and hiding are worth it anymore. Am I
right?"

I stare Ricki in the eye.

*Damn! I hate it when somebody sees right
through me like that.*

Tears start forming in my eyes, and I feel one
overflowing onto one of my cheeks. I start to
sniffle.

"Maybe," I sob.

"I got it," Ricki blurts. "You're the woman
from Pastor Kristiansen's church! I had lunch with
you in New York. I knew your accent was familiar.
It's Anna?… Angie?… Angela! Your name's
Angela, isn't it?"

I nod my head to acknowledge. Strangely,
instead of feeling afraid of Ricki knowing my
identity, I feel the beginnings of a smile trying to
break through my tears.

"I was wondering if you were going to
recognize me," I sighed. "I suppose I don't look
much like I did in New York."

"Yeah, you look like you've been having a
rough time," Ricki observed. "I remember now. You

were afraid of something when I interviewed you. I saw it in your eyes. Is that it? Is that what you're still afraid of?"

My head moves up and down silently. I'm struggling, trying to figure out how much I should reveal to Ricki, now that I've been discovered. I still feel some residual fear in my body. But I also feel like I can trust this woman. I feel stuck, not knowing what to say.

"Sounds like you still don't want to talk about it. It must be pretty bad. You had to leave your kids behind, didn't you?" she says. She's stating a fact, not judging.

I burst into tears when she mentions Julia and Nicholas, unable to keep the depths of my sadness and loneliness — and the enormous weight of my guilt — locked away any longer. Tears stream from my eyes. Rick's arms reach out and take me against her body, not saying a word, just letting me weep inconsolably. After what seems like an eternity, I finally regain some control over my sobbing and my emotions, gradually pushing them back into the dark recesses of my subconscious. I feel myself reconnecting with reality — the floodway and the warm sensation of being in Ricki's arms. I pull back from her empathic embrace.

"I saw the article you wrote about my disappearance in New York," I say. "You were still in New York?"

"Call it my second sense. I just had a feeling there was more to Pastor Soren and the WWCC than meets the eye. I saw the fear in your eyes when you wouldn't tell me anything. I knew there was a story somewhere. I just needed to hang around to find it," she answers. "Feel like talking about it now?"

I shake my head from side to side. "Not yet. Are you going to write about finding me here?" I ask.

"No," Ricki replies. "I can still write my article about the floodways without using your name." She takes my hand and looks me in the eye.

"I never finished the story about Pastor Soren and the WWCC," she says. She reaches into her pocket and pulls out her business card. She takes my hand and places the card in it.

"Here's my number in case you ever want to talk some more — off the record," she says. "Even if you just want to bounce some ideas off somebody to help figure out what you're going to do — where you're going to go."

"You promise you're not going to tell anybody I'm here?" I ask, having pushed away my tears.

"I promise," she says. "Not until you're ready to talk."

"Thanks," I answer. It's the only word I can find. I haven't said anything very meaningful to Ricki. And yet, just the very act of slowing down my thoughts and putting them into words to another person has been helpful. I feel some of my inner strength and a small amount of self-confidence returning.

"It was nice meeting you again, Angela," Ricki says, extending her hand. "Is there anything else worth seeing up ahead? Anybody else living there?"

"I don't think so," I say. "There's a lot of turns and other tunnels joining up with this one up there. It's pretty easy to get disoriented and lost."

"I'll take my chances," she says. "I don't suppose GPS will help me much, eh?"

We chuckle together at her joke. I like her sense of humor.

"Will you still be here on my way back?" Ricki asks.

"Depends," I answer. "I usually stay here until dusk, then ride my bike home."

"Am I allowed to ask where home is?" she inquires.

"Yeah, I've rented a small office space on Tropicana East. It's not very far from here by bike."

"And that's where your alter-ego hangs out?" she asks, once again rhetorically. She seems to have the slightly annoying skill of knowing the answers to questions before she even asks them. I suppose that's what makes her a good journalist.

"If you're here when I come back, do you mind if we talk some more?" she asks. I find myself answering without thinking. I can't deny I enjoyed talking to another person.

"Sure… if I'm still here," I say timidly, not wanting to sound too excited.

"I hope we connect again, Angela. But if we don't, remember to call me if you're in trouble or if you need to talk." She takes her flashlight from my shelf, then she waves to me as she backs slowly into the darkness.

"Thanks," I say, giving her a small wave in return.

Ricki's light spins around in the dark, now illuminating the far side of the tunnel.

The sound of her feet, splashing in the little streams and puddles, recedes into the distance.

"See ya later," she shouts. The darkness swallows Ricki and her light within a few seconds, and then she disappears. I find myself alone, completely engulfed in darkness again. As silence returns, the air starts reverberating with the chirping of nearby crickets. Strangely, I don't feel as despondent as I did before Ricki arrived. I feel a sense of confidence starting to return.

Maybe you can find a way out of this mess, Angela. But you're sure not going to find it down here in this tunnel.

I look up through the metal grille in the street above, realizing there's still a few hours of daylight left. Secretly, I hope Ricki manages to find her way back to my camp before I depart for the day. I start making mental notes of things I need to Google on my laptop when I get back to the office tonight. I resolve that if I can't go back to being Angela, at least I can resume building my life in Las Vegas as Anna Benz.

CHAPTER 11

RICKI WALKS beside me and my bike as we emerge from my floodway refuge into the wash beside Las Vegas Boulevard. We walk up to the Tropicana Hotel parking lot. She tells me about the few people she met on today's exploration into the floodway. Even with Ricki beside me, I feel exposed and vulnerable outside the shelter of the tunnel, as we walk from the Tropicana across to the San Remo hotel and casino.

"So, what happened that made you run, Angela? Was it something about Pastor Soren?"

I feel a lump in my throat and I try to swallow, trying to find the courage to speak — trying to decide how much to tell Ricki.

"Yes, it was Soren… and the church," I admit. "But you can't call me Angela… out here, anyway. Angela is dead. I'm Anna Benz now."

"Okay… Anna," Ricki replies. "Don't worry, I told you I'd protect your confidentiality. I take that seriously. If word gets around that I don't, I'm finished as a journalist.

I swallow again. "I believe you," I say. "But I can't tell you too much. Not right now, anyway. It's too dangerous."

"So, what are you going to do? Where are you going to go?" she asks.

"I started a business while I was living in L.A. It was going well, and I was thinking of expanding into Las Vegas," I answer, not wanting to reveal any more.

"That's cool," Ricki answered. "So you've made some contacts? You've got enough money to get things off the ground?"

"Yeah, I've got a couple of contacts, and cash isn't a problem." I notice Ricki's eyebrows go up at the mention of cash. I know she wants to ask more, but she decides against it.

"Okay, I see," she says. "I hope it works out for you."

Ricki stops and looks up at the San Remo's marquee. Seeing her look up, my eyes follow hers to the illuminated sign.

Showgirls of Illusion, Now Appearing.

"I've never heard of them before. Have you?" I asked.

"Yeah, but I'm not surprised you haven't heard of them," Ricki answered. "They're the best-kept secret on the strip. They're fantastic, but hardly anybody knows about them. I saw them a few months ago."

"What's so special?" I ask. Ricki gets a sparkle in her eye and grins.

"Do you want to see them?" Her eyes grow wide and the sparkle gets brighter. "I'll take you, and you can see for yourself."

"I don't think so," I say immediately, putting the brakes on Ricki's enthusiasm. "I'm not very good with crowds anymore."

Ricki nods her head in understanding.

"I get it," she says. "What if you see somebody you know, right? Somebody from home? Somebody you're running from? What if you see *him*?"

"Yeah," I admit. I nod my head up and down nervously.

Ricki turns and locks her eyes on mine.

"I don't know you well at all, Angela… or Anna. But I need to tell you something," she says. "Do you mind?"

I find myself swallowing hard again. I shrug my shoulders, trying to seem indifferent to what she wants to say.

"I like you. You're different from anybody else I've met in the floodways. All of the others have that vacant, faraway look in their eyes. They've all given up on life a long time ago. All I see in their eyes is hopelessness. But you're different. You're at a crossroads. You're still torn between giving up and spending the rest of your life hiding, or trying to find a way to live a normal life. And I can see you slipping over the edge into hopelessness so easily. You're right on the edge, and I don't want to see that happen to you. But I do know this. If you're going to keep from slipping over that edge, you have to do something very soon to get you moving in the right direction. You can go home, wherever that is, and hide there all night, then go back to the tunnels and live like a rat. Or you can choose to live, it's up to you. But I see it in your eyes. I know you want to live."

I look at Ricki's face and I see the genuine concern in it. She may look tough on the outside, but I see warmth and empathy beneath her hard shell.

"So what's it gonna be? Live like a hermit, or go out and have some fun tonight? It's a small theatre — only a couple hundred people at the most. And trust me, everybody's eyes are gonna be on the girls, not on you."

That's all she has to say, since I know that every word she speaks is true. I *am* living on the edge, dangerously close to regressing and turning into another Sally from San Julian Park. I swallow again. Then I lift my shoulders, push out my chest, and stand up straight. Those simple physical gestures help me to summon some of my long lost inner strength.

"Okay, let's do it. Do we buy tickets inside?"

Ricki embraces and squeezes me tight, then let's go. Her face wears a warm smile.

"I know you can do it… Anna. I'll make sure nothing bad happens. If you see somebody you know, I'll make sure you get away. You'll have fun, I promise!"

I lock my bike to a lamppost, then we wander into the lobby — me looking every bit like the derelict street person I am, and Ricki looking like she just came back from military maneuvers. I'm wearing my bike helmet, torn blue jeans, and a faded yellow t-shirt after a day of hiding out in my floodway bunker. The hair that sticks out from under my helmet is tangled and grimy, and I'm aware that we're both drawing stares from hotel staff. A concierge approaches in an effort to intercept us.

"May I help you, ladies?" he asks.

"Yes, can you point us to the box office?" Ricki replies. I feel the man's eyes staring warily at our shabby appearance, working their way up and down the two of us, from head to toe.

"Certainly," he says. He raises his right arm and points to the far left-hand corner of the lobby. "It's down the hallway, just around that corner."

"Thank you, we appreciate it," Ricki answers. We leave the young man behind us and we march toward our destination.

A young brunette with a ponytail sits behind the glass window. She also examines us suspiciously.

"You wouldn't happen to have any tickets left for tonight's late show, would you?" Ricki turns to me and smiles. "That will give us time to go home and clean up," she says. The young woman raises an eyebrow, obviously approving of our plan to clean up our appearance before attending the show.

"We do have some tickets. Seating is first come, first served. Showtime is ten o'clock, but the line-up usually starts about an hour before that. Tickets are thirty-five dollars each."

I pull a small bundle of worn bills from my jeans pocket and hand it to Ricki, who slides our money under the glass to the woman. She slides two tickets back in return.

As we turn away from the box office, I notice a poster for the *Showgirls* on the wall behind me. The group of women in the poster look like a scantily-clad burlesque review with magic props. The combination is strangely enticing, and I find myself looking forward to my first live entertainment, and my first night out in public, for a very long time. I smile at Ricki.

"Thanks for insisting," I say, and then I nod towards the poster. "I see what you meant when you said that nobody will be looking at me." I laugh and Ricki joins in.

"Do you need a ride to the show?" Ricki asks.

"No, I'm just a few minutes away from home by bike. And I have a car, so I won't have to ride my bike back here in my dress. I'll meet you here in the lobby at nine?"

"Nine it is," Ricki says. "I'll see you then."

I give Ricki a grateful hug, feeling conspicuous and awkward, and then I quickly turn and stride from the lobby. Outside, I unlock my bike, mount it, and then begin pedaling through the San Remo Hotel parking lot before taking Tropicana east to the office. Red LED warning lights on the bike are flashing, and a bright LED headlight lights the road in front of me. I'm lit up like a Christmas tree, paranoid of the busy evening traffic in Las Vegas. On the surface, I feel terrified about going out in public tonight. But beneath the fear, I feel some comfort in having Ricki's strong presence beside me. Even better, for the first time in months, I feel a sense of excitement and anticipation at the possibility of relaxing, having a girls' night out, and having some fun.

NOT HEEDING the advice of the woman in the San Remo Box Office, I only arrive at the theatre about thirty minutes before show time. I'm late, but I don't see Ricki anywhere. I find myself at the tail end of a long line-up. I feel self-conscious in one of the short dresses I'd bought in Los Angeles for my Anna Benz persona — a hot little black number with black stiletto pumps. It's been a long time since I've shown this much skin and leg.

"Anna!" I hear my name coming from behind me. "I'm so sorry I'm late. I got stuck in traffic coming into downtown. Just my luck that there was an accident on I-15."

"Don't worry," I say to Ricki. "I only just got here myself. Looks like we'll be sitting at the back."

It's only then that I notice Ricki's transformation. She's wearing tight-fitting designer jeans, a grey jacket, and a shiny sky-blue, low-cut blouse that brings out the sparkling blue color of her eyes. Enough buttons are left unfastened that I can't help but be impressed by her cleavage and the allure of her breasts. Having only recently seen her in army fatigues, I had no idea that such a stunning feminine figure was hiding underneath.

"Wow," I said, without thinking. "It's a good thing you called out to me. I never would have recognized you."

Ricki laughs spontaneously as she looks me over from top to bottom. She leans close and lowers her voice.

"I could say the same for you, girl. Nobody would ever guess you just spent a few days in the floodways either!"

We laugh together and I realize how long it's been since I've done that. I don't want it to end.

"Tell you what, you hold our place and I'll go to the bar and get us a couple of drinks. What can I get you?" Ricki inquires.

"Do they have strawberry margaritas?"

"I'm sure they do," Ricki answers. "I'll be right back."

I start feeling anxious, almost as soon as Ricki leaves me in the line-up. My eyes search the faces in the line-up, terrified that I'm going to see somebody from Cleveland or New York. I feel my chest getting heavy and tight. My eyes dart from face to face. I only start to relax after I start talking to myself, trying to convince myself that they are all total strangers. I notice that I've been holding my breath, so I start inhaling and exhaling more slowly while I talk to myself. Gradually, I feel the fear and tension relinquishing their grip on my body.

"Here we are," Ricki says, sliding back into line beside me. "Cheers!"

We each take long sips from plastic straws that stick out of the enormous Vegas-sized drinks. Within seconds, I feel the alcohol starting to seep into my bloodstream, and I welcome the relaxation it brings with it. The line-up starts inching its way toward the theatre, taking only about two or three minutes for us to reach the entrance, where an usher takes our tickets.

At first glance, the theatre is surprisingly small and intimate, seating perhaps one hundred and fifty or two hundred people. Most of the theatre is painted black, making it seem even smaller and more intimate. I look around for seats and find we only have two choices — back row, or at the far right of the front row. With Ricki by my side and alcohol seeping into my circulation, I make a bold decision.

If you're going to see a magic show, Angela, you want to see the show!

"Front row?" I say tentatively to Ricki.

"You're okay with that?" she asks in surprise. "I can sit back here if it makes you feel more comfortable."

"Now that I'm here, what the hell," I answer. "Let's live a little!"

Ricki smiles and grabs my hand, leading the way to the front row. We find ourselves getting acquainted with the couple beside us — Matt and Jessica, newlyweds from Des Moines. Fighting my paranoia of talking about myself, I introduce myself as Anna, a realtor from Las Vegas. Ricki raises her eyebrows at my new sense of daring and smiles. I let out a sigh of relief as the lights dim and the show begins.

The *Showgirls* start working the small room right away, picking audience members to participate in their illusions. I'm impressed by their talent. As advertised, the show is a fast-paced combination of burlesque and magic with well-executed magic and constant costume changes — everything from baby-doll lingerie to cowgirls in leather chaps and skimpy bras. The act moves so quickly that it's hard for me to tell how many girls are actually in the show — I think I count six or seven different women. The showgirls tease the audience with costumes that reveal more and more skin as the show progresses.

I find myself being drawn in by both their magic and their sensual striptease. It's been much too long since I've had any intimate human contact, apart from my faked sexual encounter with Soren Kristiansen eighteen months ago. I start to feel sensations between my legs that I haven't felt for a long time.

Suddenly, I find myself in the spotlight, staring at a tall *Showgirl* in a skimpy gold lamé dress. I see mostly butt cheeks and an almost non-existent gold G-string beneath her dress. My eyes scan upward from her shiny gold stilettos. She has long muscular legs, a great butt, milky-white skin, and an ample cleavage that leaves little to the imagination.

"I see someone in the crowd who secretly wants to be one of us *Showgirls*. Whadda y'all say? Do you wanna see this young lady strut her stuff?"

I feel my face turning red. I look at Ricki and see her laughing and clapping. The crowd is whistling and cheering, urging me to join the redhead on stage.

"Come on, Anna! This is your big chance!" Jessica from Des Moines shouts. Matt claps his hands high over his head and then gives a piercing whistle to urge me on. Ricki nudges me, trying to get me to take the next step. The *Showgirl* won't let it go. She's relentless.

"What's your name and where are you from, honey?"

I realize I'm trapped, with nowhere to run and hide. I find myself being swept up in the excitement of the moment.

What the hell — might as well join in and have some fun.

"Anna, from Las Vegas!" I shout.

"Anna from Las Vegas, how would you like to be a magician? Can you dance?"

I stand up and shake my head vigorously from side to side, but the redhead won't take no for an answer. She comes down from the stage, takes my hand and leads me onstage. She whispers in my ear.

"It's okay, honey. I'm Marie. I'll walk you through it, so just watch and do what I do." She turns to the crowd.

"Do y'all wanna see Anna dance?" she shouts. Once again, I hear a chorus of cheers and whistles from the audience. I see Ricki laughing and her eyes sparkling. Music starts pounding through the sound system, and Marie starts strutting a simple dance routine, her eyes signaling for me to join. Awkwardly, I start strutting to my right, almost falling off one of my black stilettos. A roar of 'oohs' and laughter fills the theatre. I follow Marie, my eyes glued to her swaying hips and bosom. My dance routine feels like it will never end. In reality, it probably only lasts about ten seconds before Marie guides me to a stop, then reaches for a prop. With great flair, she whips open a large, shiny piece of gold lamé fabric and holds it up in front of her. It covers her from the knees to her neck. Before I know it, Marie hands the reflective gold fabric to me. She leans toward me and whispers.

"Just hold it where it is, Anna, I'll do the rest. Any time I wink at you, just whip the fabric away from me. Got it?"

I nod, feeling my body tremble from the pressure. I start forgetting about the audience, focusing on my role in the act.

Don't screw up, Angela. Don't make Marie blow her tricks!

I can't see what she's doing behind the fabric. She raises her hands over her head, then extends them out, first to the right and then the left sides of the fabric, as she keeps dancing. Then I see her wink at me. I whip away the fabric, revealing Marie magically standing in front of a large box supported by four legs. I see a number of slits on all sides of the box. Marie dances to the right side of the stage, where another one of the *Showgirls*, a blonde woman dressed in gold lamé like Marie, and carrying four swords, dances onstage with her. Marie whispers to me again.

"You're doing great, Anna. Keep it up! This is Tara. If I disappear, just do as she says."

Marie opens the box, then spins it around so the crowd can see that it's empty and there's nothing underneath. Then she climbs in and curls her long, lean body into a compact ball. Tara motions for me to close and padlock the doors to the box. The music continues to pound out a rock rhythm, and Tara motions for me to dance back and forth across the stage with her as the crowd claps and dances along with us.

When we arrive back at the box, Tara takes one of the swords and thrusts it through one of the slots in the box. The crowd gasps, then cheers. Tara hands me the three remaining swords and nods in my direction. I know what she wants me to do, but I plead *no* with my eyes. She just smiles and nods again. I take one sword and push it tentatively through the slot. It sticks and I meet with resistance.

You're really stabbing Marie. This isn't working!

My eyes beg Tara to make me stop. She smiles and nods again. I push the next sword into another slot, feeling the same revolting physical sensation of resistance. Tara nods again, and I push the last sword home. I feel ill. In my mind, I see tomorrow's headlines.

'San Remo Illusion Goes Wrong!'

Tara produces the piece of gold fabric, giving it an exaggerated wave again in front of the box, before holding it still in front of her. She leans towards me and whispers.

"I'll count to three, then I want you to whip away the sheet on four. Understand?"

I give a timid, uncertain nod, and Tara smiles back at me. She holds her hands high above the gold fabric, clapping and holding a microphone as she and the crowd keep dancing to the pounding beat.

"Okay, everybody. Count to three with me, and we'll bring Marie back!"

The crowd roars and whistles in approval.

"One… two… three…" Tara nods and mouths, *'four'*.

I whip away the sheet. There stands Tara, wearing only her gold heels and G-string, her large breasts and rosy nipples bobbing in time to the music before my eyes. The crowd roars. Men and women alike scream and whistle their approval.

I gasp in surprise. The box hasn't changed. The doors are still locked closed and the sword handles still protrude from the box. Tara passes the gold

fabric back to me with her usual panache, and I
hold it in front of her again.

"Okay, everybody. Let's try it again! This time,
I need you to shout louder. Do you think you can do
that?"

Tara has the mob eating out of her hands now. I
get the sense that she's stalling as she stirs the
audience to greater heights.

"Let's do it! One… two… three." Tara looks at
me and nods…

I'm starting to get the hang of doing this. I
whip the gold sheet away with as much flair as I
can summon, revealing Tara in her gold stilettos and
G-string. The swords are gone; the box is empty.
Then I notice another pair of legs behind Tara. She
moves aside and Marie struts forward, sans dress,
wearing only her gold heels and G-string. The
audience goes wild.

Marie winks at me as she struts forward and
takes my hand. I'm stunned by reappearance. The
sudden, unexpected beauty of her nearly-naked
body leaves me feeling breathless. Her muscular
legs and butt are hard. Her breasts are smaller than
Tara's, but higher and more firm. Her skin is milky-
white, without a sign of cellulite on her thighs or
butt. Her lithe figure is simply breathtaking.
Judging by the roar of the audience, I'm not the
only person in the theatre who appreciates her great
beauty.

Damn! That's not fair. How can anybody have a body like that!

Marie and I stand side by side and she holds my hand. Tara joins me on the other side, holding my other hand. Both *Showgirls* look at me, smile, then turn to the audience and begin to bow. The non-verbal tug on my hands tells me I'm supposed to bow with them. After we take our bows, we stand facing the appreciative audience. I suddenly realize I'm not afraid anymore.

I see Ricki in the audience, laughing hysterically, applauding, and smiling back at me.

Marie leads me back to my seat, then leans forward and gives me a quick kiss on each cheek, then whispers in my ear.

"You did great, Anna. Enjoy the rest of the show."

I squeeze her hand and smile at her.

"Thanks, I'm sure I will," I say, giving her an appreciative smile.

I turn to Ricki, unable to wipe the grin off my face or to stop laughing. The feeling is exhilarating.

"You were great!" Ricki shouts over the applause. "I knew you could do it!"

Marie and Tara make their way back to the stage, and they're replaced by five other *Showgirls*, who keep up the pace by moving quickly into the next illusion. This time, all five are topless. I find myself clapping and chanting with Ricki and the rest of the audience, urging them on. I don't want the performance to end.

I FEEL EMPTY as I walk from the San Remo Hotel to my Honda Civic and climb inside. I'm just coming down from the natural high of fun, excitement, and laughter from the show. I don't want the feelings to end. I also feel empty as I remember leaving Ricki behind in the lobby. It's the first fun I've had with another human for far too long. In my mind, I replay our embrace and our promise to keep in touch. We laugh and Ricki makes me promise that our next meeting won't be in the floodway.

I let a long breath escape from my lungs as I relax into the driver's seat. I'm glad Ricki had the impulse to see the *Showgirls of Illusion*. The show started me thinking.

Angela, you haven't done anything for fun in over six months. It's no wonder you feel so sad and guilty — you're not doing anything positive in your life right now. You need to fix that right away. You need to get Anna Benz going, and you need to get serious about looking for properties tomorrow.

Then I start smiling, as I remember my reaction to seeing Ricki's dramatic feminine transformation and Marie's sensuous, nearly naked body.

Dammit, girl. It's been way too long since you've seen anybody naked or felt anybody touch you. You really do need to find somebody and get yourself laid!

CHAPTER 12

IT'S BEEN a busy day. For the first time in weeks, I finally feel like I have a sense of direction for my life again. I spent the day with a realtor, scouring the areas around UNLV for student housing listings. There were some good properties with lots of potential, so I'm feeling optimistic about breaking into the Las Vegas market.

My mind is wandering again. I find myself Googling the CBS news report from Palm Desert, where I saw my portrait hanging in the background. I haven't dared look at the news clip since I first saw it, about three weeks ago, but my curiosity has finally got the best of me. I click on the *Play* button and start watching the report again. I'm getting over the shock of seeing myself on the news, but my curiosity about the mysterious photographer escalates daily.

Who is she? Why was she in San Julian Park last fall? What happened at the Palm Desert estate?

I start following a trail of links from the CBS website, garnering background information on the fiasco in Palm Desert.

Francesca Capellini, married to successful Parisian art agent and dealer, Philippe Morel. Co-owner of Chateau Eden, a nudist retreat in Palm Springs. Capellini's husband lures two guests, Dan and Michelle Whitney, from Chateau Eden to the Palm Desert estate. The two couples swap and start dabbling in kinky sex. Michelle Whitney is shot by Morel when the Whitneys try to escape. Capellini drowns Morel. You're kidding — she drowns her own husband?

I click on a few more links to find out more about Capellini, but she seems to have stayed in her husband's shadow over the years. Another link catches my eye. I click on it and find myself reading an article in the *Los Angeles Times.*

'Capellini Hires Expert on Battered Wife Defense'.

I read on, discovering that Capellini's husband, Morel, was apparently a real control freak. I start feeling sorry for Capellini and the two victims.

Dan Whitney — psychologist — sounds like it was his wife that wanted to start swinging with Morel. I feel sorry for Whitney, but why didn't he just say no to his wife? Seems kind of odd if you ask me.

I find myself starting at photos of the two survivors, Capellini and Dan Whitney. I have to admit they're both attractive and fit. The article goes on to say that Whitney is now living at the nudist resort with Capellini.

Have they really hit it off? Maybe they're both just in a state of shock. Neither one of them seems to have much family. Maybe they only have each other right now.

The more I read, the more I find my fascination with Whitney and Capellini growing. It's odd, because I don't have the faintest idea why. My biggest concern should be my own safety, now that my face has appeared on every major newscast in America. I wonder if Momma and Papa noticed? I wonder if they know I'm alive now?

I find myself wanting to know more about the tragedy, especially about Whitney and Capellini, so I keep searching the web for more information. Inevitably, my research brings me back to the CBS news video, and I find myself gazing at my own portrait, staring into my own eyes again. Before long, I find myself reliving that afternoon in San Julian Park, once again feeling the sense of panic I felt while Capellini stalked me with her camera. Suddenly, I feel like I'm back on East 5th Street in Los Angeles, running again from a danger I don't understand.

I don't remember how long I ran that day. I waited for nightfall, taking advantage of the darkness to wind my way through the streets of East Los Angeles. I don't know how I did it, but I managed to find my way back to the office I'd just rented on South Figueroa. I remember locking the deadbolt and not setting foot outside for three full days. It was a week before I dared venture back into Skid Row.

I'm vaguely aware that my right foot is vibrating up and down rapidly. I realize I'm not back in Los Angeles. I'm in my new office on Tropicana Avenue in Las Vegas. My eyes focus on the laptop screen in front of me. I'm still staring at the portrait — staring into my own eyes. I imagine I hear my own voice talking to me from the photograph.

Do you really want to keep living this way, Angela? You might be safe, living like a rat in a sewer during the day, and hiding out in this hole at night. But is this any kind of life?

I gaze into the background of the CBS news video, and I find myself thinking of Francesca Capellini and Dan Whitney again. I now believe, more than ever, that the road back to my family is somehow linked to the photo of me that Capellini captured on her old SLR in San Julian Park. Now, when I look at the portrait, I'm beginning to see something else — an Angela that is strong — a survivor. And deep inside, I'm starting to feel something stirring that I haven't felt for almost two years. Motivation.

I make another resolution with myself. It's time to start moving forward with my life.

Keep your eyes and ears open, Angela. An opportunity will come. Something that will help you get your old life back again. You'll know it when you see it. Just be patient — it will come.

I'm aware that patience isn't my strong suit. Nevertheless, I vow to stop hiding in the floodway. I know that I can't keep living my life as Anna Benz or Grace Wagner forever. I need to find a way to start seeing the world through my own eyes, and to start living my own life again. And I vow to resume working on that goal tomorrow, even if it has to be as Anna Benz, for the time being.

I'M STANDING at the sink in my Tropicana office's tiny bathroom after spending the day looking at some promising student properties. I'm hot and sticky after an unusually warm spring day, treating myself to a sponge bath. After three weeks of keeping myself clean this way, I'd pay just about anything to have a nice long bath.

You've got the money, girl. Why don't you treat yourself and spend the night in a hotel?

I resolve to think about it some more.

I have the TV on in the background for company. My mind is wandering yet again. My night out with Ricki made me realize that I've been spending too much time on my own, with little to do but ruminate on the current state of my life. I decide that hearing human voices from the TV right now is better than silence.

I'm standing naked in front of the bathroom mirror. I'm no *Showgirl of Illusion*. On the other hand, I certainly haven't been overeating for the past eighteen months. I may not be in prime physical condition, but I'm slim and I decide that I'm not exactly unattractive.

As I apply hot water to my body and scrub with a facecloth, it feels comforting and warm at first. But the feeling is short-lived, replaced by a brisk chill as the warm liquid rapidly evaporates into the cool dry air. I feel the fine hairs standing on end all over my body. My nipples pop out, becoming plump and firm.

The monotonous cycle of daytime TV chatter and advertisements is interrupted by the announcement of an urgent news bulletin. My ears pick up on the change of tone, suddenly becoming attuned where only seconds ago they were habituated to the constant racket.

'This just in... an Amber Alert has been issued across the Western States for a missing boy, who is feared to have been kidnapped by his father. Five-year-old Jonah Kristiansen is thought to be in the custody of his father, Pastor Soren Kristiansen,

enigmatic leader of the World-Wide Community of Christ...'

A chill races down my spine as I hear those two words — *Soren Kristiansen*. I drop the facecloth in the sink and race to the TV. Completely naked, I find myself staring at the two photos being flashed on the TV screen. The first face I see smiling out at me from my antiquated portable television, is that of a respected pastor of a growing evangelical church based in Victoria, British Columbia. The second face, a young boy, I recognize from the family portrait hanging in Soren's New York office. I watch in disbelief.

'Those who know Pastor Kristiansen are giving testimonials to the man, hoping that nothing sinister has happened to him or his son,' the announcer says. The station cuts to clips of church members giving testimonials to Pastor Soren's outstanding character.

'He's a loving husband and father — a man of God whose mission in life is to spread God's word and to help others who are less fortunate,' declares one woman. *'I'm sure there's a reasonable explanation for what has happened. The Pastor Soren I know could never be involved in child abduction. He's happily married,'* says a man from his congregation.

The Amber Alert covers the entire western half of Canada and the United States, but there has been no sign yet of Soren Kristiansen or his son Jonah. It isn't possible, they all say, that Pastor Kristiansen could have kidnapped his own son. Surely the authorities must be wrong.

But I know differently. The Soren Kristiansen I know is a man of many faces. He's a chameleon. In him, I see the cunning, calculating face of somebody who is always looking for a way to get whatever he wants from whomever he comes in contact with. In his smug, disingenuous smile, I see a man who secretly laughs at others, even while his admirers swoon from being in his presence. I should know. I was one of those admirers at one time.

I know his face from another time and another place. It's been less than two years since I fled from New York and went underground to escape his nefarious grasp. I'm weary from running and hiding — from constantly looking over my shoulder, in case Soren or his associates are on my trail. I know I did it to protect my two children, but I'm worn out from the constant need to be vigilant every second of my life. I feel a chill surge through my spine, recognizing it as fear. It's the same feeling I had when I first realized how dangerous a man he is, and what he is capable of doing to those who challenge him.

My thoughts are interrupted by the voice of the African-American woman who is giving the latest update on the investigation into the boy's disappearance. The young boy's photo remains prominently displayed in the upper right corner of the screen, as the newscast continues.

'Police in Victoria, British Columbia, won't comment on reports that they were following up on complaints about irregularities in donations to Pastor Kristiansen's online ministry, The World-Wide Community of Christ, at the time of the young boy's disappearance,' the woman reported. *'This isn't the first controversy to tarnish Pastor Kristiansen's image. He was also implicated in the disappearance of a Cleveland woman in 2004. Although he admitted to having a sexual encounter with the woman, he has repeatedly denied having anything to do with her disappearance. Rumors have also been circulating that Pastor Kristiansen's marriage has been on the rocks over the past year.'*

So, it's about time that they're finally catching up with you, Soren. Now it's your turn to be on the run.

My mind starts wandering, as I realize the implications of the news bulletin for me. My eyes roam around the seedy second-floor office. It isn't that the office space is old. Nothing in Las Vegas is very old. But large parts of the city, like the area surrounding my office, are run-down and tired. These are the areas of the city that house the thousands of poorly-paid drones who clean hotel rooms, cook in kitchens, and serve drinks to throngs of tourists who visit the city each year. I laugh to myself, realizing that the dirty, neutral-colored walls and the stained overhead ceiling tiles make the office look as tired as I feel. The aging AC unit in the roof vibrates and growls as it struggles to cope with the rising late-afternoon temperature in the office.

The room is sparsely furnished with the furniture I'd brought with me from Los Angeles. A medium-sized safe, standing about four feet in height and anchored to the wall with heavy bolts, is grey, shiny, and the only new item in the room. It holds the documents for my two identities, Anna Benz and Grace Wagner, as well as a substantial amount of cash for emergencies, in case I have to go on the run again. The brand new safe stands in stark contrast to the well-used office and the rest of its furnishings. A small wooden table, with a microwave oven sitting on top, stands against the wall on the opposite side of the room from the safe. Beside it, a small bar fridge hums. Those small appliances have allowed me to come out from my floodway hideout at the end of each day to have a hot meal.

Against the back wall of the dingy room, to the right of the office's entrance, a solitary wooden door, painted the same nondescript color as the walls, marks the small bathroom. Lacking a shower, this is where I settle for sponge baths to wash away the odor and grime of the underground floodways, where I've spent much of my time since coming to Las Vegas. On the left side of the entrance, half a dozen dresses, skirts, assorted blouses and camisoles hang on plastic hangers. The small wardrobe was sufficient for my excursions into the world of business in Los Angeles as Anna Benz, and should continue to serve Anna well in Las Vegas.

The centerpiece of the room is my laptop computer, which sits atop a medium-sized contemporary office table from IKEA. The laptop is my lifeline to the world, and my connection to the intricate network of financial transactions I wove to launder and hide the small fortune I stole from Soren. An aging rolling office chair sits in front of the table and computer. My old portable television perches atop two red plastic milk crates that I liberated from behind the convenience store on the ground floor below.

The office, along with its mélange of furnishings, has been enough to meet my simple needs. But I realize that the time is drawing near when I'm going to have to abandon the space and leave Las Vegas. The seed of a newer, better plan is germinating in my mind.

You can't keep running and hiding like this, Angela. You might be the only one who can help track Soren and find the boy. He won't be expecting you to be coming after him. He's not your ordinary run-of-the-mill child abductor. He has almost unlimited resources. Even worse, he has connections in high places that the police can't even imagine. But you know how he thinks. You have the ability to follow his digital footprints. He's a dangerous adversary, and you're going to have to be extremely cautious. But you're going to have to hunt him down if you ever hope to get your life back.

My attention is grabbed again by the newscast. They're running video of a blonde woman with short, wavy hair. I instantly recognize the face from the family portrait in Soren's office. It's Anika Kristiansen, Soren's wife and the boy's mother, appearing in front of reporters. Beside Anika, a handsome brown-haired man stands with his arm wrapped around the woman's upper back, his hand resting on her shoulder for support. I feel confused. I know I've seen the man's face before in a different context, but I can't make a connection at the moment.

'Jonah, honey, I love you and miss you very much,' Anika says, sniffling into reporter's microphones, tears clearly visible in her bloodshot eyes. *'We'll have you home very soon, honey.'*

Anika sniffles again and tries to swallow, struggling to find words.

'Soren, for Jonah's sake, I beg you to turn yourself in so he can come home. And to the public, both in British Columbia and the Pacific Northwest, if you see the man or the boy in these pictures, please contact your local police immediately.'

Anika breaks down, sobbing uncontrollably. The brown-haired man puts both of his arms around her to console her. The newscast cuts back to the local news anchor. New video of a construction accident at one of the huge hotel construction sites on the Las Vegas Strip, replaces the Amber Alert story.

I realize that tears have filled my own eyes as I watched Anika's emotional plea. I know too well the pain of not being able to be with my children. It's been almost two years since I chose to disappear, leaving my own two children, Julia and Nicholas, in the custody of my aging parents in Cleveland. My heart aches from not being able to contact them, or to tell them I'm alive. But for their sake, my disappearance had to look suspicious. It was best for the world to assume I was dead.

Choking back my tears, I turn my attention to the laptop in front of me to distract myself. Since my disappearance, I haven't dared to contact anybody from my former life, let alone access the intricate corporate computer network of Soren's financial empire. It would be suicide to use my old access codes.

If you're going to find out what he's up to, you're going to have to find a way to hack into the WWCC system.

I skip back into the bathroom and slip on a pair of sweatpants and a t-shirt, my cold nipples straining against the tight cotton shirt. I sit down in my rolling chair, lean back and stretch, letting my mind mull over potential solutions to my problem. After a moment, a smile spreads across my face. My hand starts sliding a mouse around on the table, clicking buttons and typing hurriedly on the keypad.

It's simple, Angela. Just hit him the same way he hits his unsuspecting church members — with an email message that he'll never suspect. First you need to search for domain names...

I type in the domain name for *World-Wide Community of Christ.* As expected, the domain search engine tells me the name is taken, but it gives me a number of useful suggestions for similar domain names. I try again, this time typing *"World_Wide"* instead of *"World-Wide"*.

"Voilà!" I say, smiling to myself. "It's available."

I set to work, setting up a bogus website and email server, hoping to catch Soren off-guard. Once that's done, I set up a fake user account in my name. When I'm finished, I have a mail server that looks almost identical to the WWCC mail server.

Next, I search my laptop for the video clips I took of Soren outside the Four Seasons hotel in Beverly Hills. Once I've located them, I scan through the clips, seeing Soren raising his head and staring at me in my sunglasses and ball cap, as I hide my face behind the video camera. It's only now that I realize how close I came to having him recognize me. I shiver again, then I set to work, editing a few clips into a thirty-second video of my brief encounter with Soren. Thirty seconds should be long enough for my purposes. After setting up an account on a new video sharing service called *YouTube*, I upload my movie onto the internet.

While the movie clip is uploading, I carefully compose my email message:

To: Soren Kristiansen
From: Angela Baranyi
Subject: I'm watching you!

Hello, Soren. I'm sending you this message, and a link to an interesting video, as a friendly reminder that I'm always watching you. I just want to make sure you're keeping your end of our bargain. I hope you're continuing to do everything in your power to make sure that Julia, Nicholas, and my parents stay healthy and safe. I think the linked video clip will impress upon you how easy it would be for me to harm you any time I wish.

Angela.

As the video finishes loading, I attach a hyperlink to the email message. What Soren doesn't know, is that I've also planted instructions within the hyperlink to plant a Trojan virus on his computer.

At last, with one final click of my mouse, my mail message hurtles out into cyberspace. If all goes well, Soren will open the link when he gets a chance. If he's on the run, it may take days for him to open the email. But when he does, my Trojan will plant itself deep within the Windows Registry on his computer while he's watching the video. Once planted, the Trojan will destroy virtually all traces of itself.

I feel a sense of satisfaction. Along with it, I feel a smile on my face. It's been far too long since I've enjoyed those sensations of pride and self-confidence. It could be days until Soren logs into his laptop, if ever. Once the Trojan starts doing its job, it will start creating a clone of Soren's hard drive on the new external hard drive that's connected to my laptop. And once the clone is complete, I can reboot my computer and search every file on his computer, including his browser history. But it could take days, or even weeks, for the synchronization to complete.

All you can do now, Angela, is wait, hope, and be patient. Game on, Pastor Kristiansen! Let's just see which one of us is best at hiding and changing our face. I dare you to find me before I find you!

I lean back in the flimsy office chair, my mind drifting again as I stretch. It's hard to believe that it's only been a month since I'd seen myself in the portrait on the Palm Springs TV news. That's when I first knew that my underground life was going to start unravelling.

Something suddenly clicks in my mind and I jerk myself upright in my chair.

That face — in the news report with Anika Kristiansen — that's where you've seen him before!

My fingers go to work, quickly bringing up the news article and video of the CBS newscast about the spectacular deaths of Philippe Morel and Michelle Whitney in Palm Springs. I search through the article until I come to the photos of the key players in the debacle. I instantly recognize the picture of Dan Whitney as the man who was supporting Anika Kristiansen at today's news conference. The photos of Dan Whitney and Francesca Capellini are side by side in the news article. I feel confused.

How the hell does Whitney know Anika Kristiansen? The Palm Springs deaths don't have anything to do with today's Amber Alert, so what's the link? How could you be so unlucky as to have him involved with both the Capellini woman and Anika Kristiansen? How could you have known Capellini would take your picture? How could you know that your face would be flashed on TV for the whole world to see?

I feel confused. It causes me to fall back inside myself, feeling my inner turmoil again. On one hand, I feel a part of me that wants to be strong again, like I did when I moved to New York, and later when I finally decided that I couldn't continue to work for Soren. It's the part of me that wants to hunt him down and help bring him to justice. But on the other hand, there's a part of me that's afraid. Afraid of confronting him again, and afraid of what he might do to Nicholas and Julia. If Soren can kidnap his own child, what else is he capable of doing? But more than anything, I'm afraid that I'll fail. And that frightened part of me is still telling me to keep running and hiding.

I replay the Palm Springs news clip again, freezing it so I can stare into Capellini's portrait of me, and gaze into my own eyes again. I see the fear and distrust in those eyes that I felt at the time. That portrait brings me face to face with what I've become over the past two years and what I'm feeling now. I've become a completely different Angela, and I don't like what I see. I've become weak and afraid.

I think back to how I finally managed to bounce back from the fear and lack of confidence — and from the depression — after divorcing David. Then a thought occurs to me and it makes me laugh. Maybe I do have to thank Soren for one thing, after all. If it hadn't been for him, I wouldn't have discovered that stronger, more confident part of myself in the first place. I wouldn't have started to feel like I could survive on my own.

You were finally starting to believe in yourself when you worked for him and when you left New York, Angela. Look at the guts it took to steal his money and to meet with those bankers in Geneva. Something happened to you between the time you landed in Toronto and when you arrived in Los Angeles. You started out as a survivor, and you ended up cowering and hiding like a sewer rat.

I start feeling a familiar weight descending on my shoulders and chest again. I recognize it as my old friend — guilt. I find myself struggling to breathe at the same time that I'm trying to choke back my tears again. This time, I'm not successful. The dam breaks and tears flood down my face. I finally give in to all of my conflicting emotions, and feel completely overwhelmed. I push my laptop away and lay my head on my arms. Sadness and loneliness wash over me like a tidal wave. I weep uncontrollably until I'm exhausted and my eyelids grow heavy. The flow of tears only ceases when I finally cry myself to sleep.

CHAPTER 13

A DOOR SLAMS and I'm sitting bolt upright in my chair. I'm still half asleep, disoriented, trying to get my bearings. My office seems strange and my mind tries to make sense of where I am. Then images start creeping into my consciousness — seemingly random fragments of dreams start rising to the surface. I start chuckling to myself. Then I start laughing hysterically. Somebody downstairs must have slammed a door and woken me abruptly from my sleep. The fragments of a dream are starting to coalesce in my conscious mind, and the bizarre plot has me in stitches.

What is going on in your brain, Angela! Where the hell did that nonsense come from!

I put my mind in *Replay* mode, trying to bring all of the fragments together into something coherent, then I try to remember it from the beginning. It appears that I am living in a complex of condo apartments, somewhere in the tropics. The apartments are clustered around a central swimming pool and patio area. I know it isn't Las Vegas, because it's hot, but far more humid than Nevada. Another wave of laughter washes over me, as I see myself in the dream. I'm dressed in a red bustier that leaves nothing to the imagination, and I see that it's pushing my boobs up almost up to my chin. Black thong panties, black fishnet stockings, and black high heels complete the ensemble, making me look like a cocktail waitress in a Las Vegas casino. By itself, this fact wouldn't be so funny. But in the dream, I'm wearing this outfit while standing in front of the stove, cooking supper!

I recall hearing the sounds of arguing neighbors while I'm cooking — a man and a woman having a heated domestic debate somewhere upstairs. Between the heat from the stove and the humidity in the air, I feel the need to cool off. I laugh again as I remember freeing my bosom from the bustier and continuing to cook — topless!

The arguing from upstairs gets louder. The woman is in great despair, while the man's voice is angry and threatening. Their escalating confrontation makes me feel nervous, and I suddenly get the urge to intervene. Forgetting my state of partial undress, I leave my apartment and venture out onto the patio. An old man and woman sit in patio chairs beside a table, shaded by a patio umbrella. They look vaguely familiar. After a few seconds, I suddenly recognize them, and I instinctively cover my breasts with my arms and hands.

"Momma. Papa. What are you doing here!" I shout in dismay.

"What are *you* doing," Momma says. "You're not thinking of trying to break up that argument, are you?"

"Put your clothes back on and come home," Papa pleads. "Julia and Nicholas need you."

I feel embarrassed, and I feel guilty about being away from my children, but I also feel compelled to find out why the couple are arguing.

"It's okay, Papa. Everything will be alright. Tell Nicholas and Julia that I love them and I'll be home soon. I just have some business I need to take care of first."

I kiss Momma on the cheek and Papa on the top of the head, then I run to a set of stairs that ascends to apartments on the second floor. I follow the sounds of shouting along a long exterior corridor, until I come to an apartment where the sliding glass patio door is wide open.

I'm shocked when I look inside. Instead of one man and one woman, there are two men and a woman. To my dismay, I realize that the two men are Soren Kristiansen and Dan Whitney. The woman is Soren's wife, Anika. Their heads turn when they see me standing, partially naked, in the doorway. Soren's face turns red with rage and his eyes open wide when he sees me.

"You!" Soren shouts. "What the hell do *you* want! You've already taken my money. Do you want to take my son away too? I should put my hands around your throat and put you out of your misery!"

I look around their apartment, but there's no sign of a young boy. I know I should feel embarrassed by my state of partial nudity, and I should feel afraid of Soren. Yet, strangely, I feel empowered. I suddenly feel confident in myself. I'm one of the *Showgirls of Illusion*.

"Don't be foolish, Soren," Whitney says, trying to play the role of referee. "You're not going to hurt anybody. You would only be hurting yourself and the boy."

"Soren, just tell us where Jonah is," Anika begs. "We can work out an agreement so Jonah can have both of us in his life."

Anika turns to me and frowns.

"Who are you, and why are you naked?"

I look at myself, and sure enough, somehow I've lost all of the rest of my clothes, except for the black high heels. Apart from that I'm totally naked. Yet, the more naked and vulnerable I become, the more empowered I feel.

"Are you the slut that Soren screwed in New York?" Anika continues. "We don't need your help. Go back where you came from. You've caused enough trouble already. Isn't that right, Dan?"

Whitney's eyes meet mine. I feel an eerie shiver shoot down my spine. It's like our eyes have met before — like he's stared into my eyes sometime in the past. But, I know we've never met.

"Don't I know you from somewhere? Aren't you one of those magic girls?" he asks.

"No. My name is Angela — not Anna or Grace. I'm Angela. This is the real me. I just want to go back to Cleveland," I say.

The real-life me starts laughing again at the absurdity of the dream and my role in it. But I realize there's more. My memory is on a roll and the dream fragments keep falling into place.

"You've got two children in Cleveland, don't you?" Anika asks. "Why don't you go back and take care of them?"

"I can't," I answer. "I can't see them until I help you find Jonah. That's just the way it is."

Soren, who has been pacing back and forth during my conversation with Anika and Dan, steps between me and Dan and Anika. His face is red and I see the muscles flexing in his jaw and neck. He pushes his body against me and puts his face directly in front of mine.

"You'll never find Jonah," he hisses, trying to intimidate me with his physical presence and the venom in his voice. He leers at my breasts, trying to make me feel self-conscious. "And you'll never find me either, once I leave here. Now put on your clothes, and get out of here before I do something you'll regret, you naked little whore!"

Strangely, Soren's leer and his angry words don't make me feel uncomfortable. Instead, my sense of empowerment continues to grow stronger.

Back in the present, I can't stop chuckling. I shake my head slowly from side to side, entertained by the bizarreness of my subconscious nocturnal fantasy. With its huge cast of characters, the dream feels like a remake of *It's a Mad, Mad, Mad, Mad, World*. And yet, despite its bizarre departures from reality, I feel it starting to have an emotional effect. I try to recall more fragments and details.

"I don't care if you all see me naked. I don't have anything to hide anymore. This is the real me. No more costumes or fake identities. All I want to do is find Jonah and be free to be me again."

I turn my bare butt to the other three characters of my apparition, and amble confidently out of the room and down the corridor to the staircase. When I reach the bottom, I realize that Mamma and Papa are no longer sitting in the chairs by the pool. Instead, the two patio chairs are occupied by Marie, from *Showgirls of Illusion*, and my new friend, reporter Ricki Marshall. Both women are totally nude, soaking up the last warm rays of late afternoon sun.

"What are you doing here," I say in surprise, wondering where Mamma and Papa had gone.

"We're just here to cheer you on," Ricki says. "We're proud of you for standing up to the Pastor up there."

"Yeah," Marie the showgirl says. "It's good to see you take off your disguise and come out of your shell."

"Thanks to the two of you," I say. I feel my eyes gazing at the two naked women in front of me. Somehow, I feel a debt of gratitude to them, and I want to get to know them better. I also start feeling a warm, damp sensation beginning to grow between my legs.

"Would you like to meet us for drinks after my show tonight?' Marie asks.

"I'd love to," I answer. "But I have to find a missing boy first. I hope you don't mind. Maybe another time?"

Marie and Ricki look at each other and shrug their shoulders. Ricki turns to me and answers.

"Whenever you're ready," she says. "We'll still be here."

I wander back into the apartment and dress myself so I can go back to cooking dinner. As I pull the stockings up and finish covering my breasts with the bustier, I hear a tiny sniffling sound coming from the patio behind me.

I turn around and see the chairs where first Momma and Papa, then Marie and Ricki, had been sitting. One of the chairs is now occupied by a blond boy who appears to be five or six years of age. He looks frightened and lonely. I walk up to him, kneel down in front of him, and take his hand.

"What's your name?" I ask.

"I'm Jonah — Jonah Kristiansen," he says. "What's your name?"

"My name is Angela."

"Is that like angel, but with an 'a' on the end?"

"Yes it is," I say, laughing.

"You have a pretty voice," he says. "It sounds like you're singing when you talk."

"Thanks, Jonah. Where's your mommy and daddy?"

"My daddy's hiding, and I don't know where my mommy is. I'm scared. Daddy says Mommy is one of the bad people. Is that true? I just want to be with her."

I see tears in Jonah's eyes, but I see him trying to be strong.

"Listen to me, Jonah. Your mommy loves you very much. She's looking for you, and I'm going to help her find you. Would you like that?"

In the distance, I hear the man and woman shouting at each other. I hear Soren stomping around angrily, and I hear another man trying to calm everybody down. Then I hear something smash against a wall.

The real-life me is still laughing at the absurdity of the dream. Even though both Jonah and

I hear the adults arguing nearby in the dream, we both seem unable to recognize them as his parents. Since I came down from the second floor, I no longer recognize them as Soren, Anika, and Dan. It's like the dream has two disjoint realities on the first and second floors of the condo complex.

Jonah appears to be puzzled and looks up towards the second floor where the shouting is coming from. A look of concern and fear crosses his face as he hears the escalation in Soren's rage. He slides off the chair so he's standing in front of me, then he throws his arms around my neck and shoulders and squeezes me as hard as he can.

"You promise?" he asks.

"Yes, I promise," I answer. "Wherever you go, you keep watching for me. I'll be watching over you. When you see me close by, you'll know that your mommy is getting close, and she's going to find you. Okay?"

Jonah nods his head up and down, then brushes away the last of his tears. He reaches out to shake my hand…

… *BANG*…

THE REAL-LIFE ME realizes it must have been the slamming of a door downstairs in the convenience store, coming at that very moment in my dream, that must have wakened me.

I giggle one last time and shake my head in amazement, wondering how my brain could have concocted the bizarre plot with such a huge cast of characters from recent events in my life. But my mind won't let it go, as if it's using the dream to work through my dilemmas and conflicts, trying to send me a message.

The more I think about the dream, the message grows more clear. I can't shake the feeling deep inside, that the only way I can ever see Julia and Nicholas again, is to reunite Jonah with Anika Kristiansen. And as that feeling grows, I feel more and more compelled to find a way to help Anika and Dan Whitney find the boy.

In the back of my mind, I still hear the voice of my guilt — the voice that has been plaguing me for the past two years.

Look what you've done to Julia and Nicholas, and to Momma and Papa. What kind of a mother abandons her children, leaving them with her parents? Don't they deserve to have their mother and their daughter?

But that voice is slowly growing weaker. Instead, I feel myself gathering strength and a resolve to fight back against my voices of guilt and hopelessness. I feel all of the parts of my identity that have been missing for so long, starting to come together — Angela the nurturing mother, Angela the loving daughter, and Angela the faithful friend. And for the first time, I hear those voices talking to me in unison, as one voice.

Julia and Nicholas DO deserve their mother, and Momma and Papa deserve their daughter! Dori deserves to have you back as a best friend. You deserve to be a mother, a daughter, and a best friend again. You don't have to run forever. You can't keep running and hiding. You must find a way to stop!

I look up and see my laptop on the table. The video news report of Dan Whitney's Palm Desert nightmare is still frozen on the screen. I find myself staring back into my own eyes in that portrait in the background again. This time, I stare past the fear and distrust. Behind those emotions, I see the Angela who has always managed to find a way to move forward, and to survive. I see Angela the mother, Angela the daughter, and Angela the friend in my eyes. I find myself whispering to the Angela in the photograph.

Thank you for finding me. I won't let you down. I'll find a way to make it back home. It might not be right now, but I'll find a way.

CHAPTER 14

THE LIGHTS of Las Vegas flash and twinkle, and the Luxor's searchlight wanders back and forth through the night sky. Ricki and I sit in the dark in my Tropicana office, gazing out the window at the neon spectacle in front of us and working our way through a bottle of Chardonnay. I've spent most of the day thinking about my dream, concluding that continuing my life as Anna Benz, property developer, is a dead end. I've also concluded that my only option for getting my life back, is to help find Jonah Kristiansen and reunite him to his mother.

I found the guts to phone Ricki and invite her over, deciding to allow her into my life and to tell her my story. We've just finished watching the news video of the Palm Desert fiasco, freezing the action when it came to showing my portrait in the background. I connected the dots for her, telling her about that day in San Julian Park when the Capellini woman took the photographs. Then we watched the news videos of the Amber Alert for Jonah and Soren Kristiansen, and the press conference with Anika Kristiansen and Dan

Whitney. I haven't had a chance yet to tell her all of the gory details of my time working for Soren in New York.

"Wow," Ricki sighs. She takes another long sip of wine. "I sure regret not finishing that story on Soren and the WWCC. It looks like I was right when I started looking into the church's finances. Now every news service in the country is going to be on it."

I swirl the Chardonnay around in my plastic cup, then I take a satisfying sip.

"Yeah," I reply. "But now you have something that nobody else has."

Ricki gazes at my face, seeing my satisfied smile. "Why do I get the feeling that 'something' is you? I don't even know the half of your story yet, do I? That's why you were so scared when I met with you in New York, isn't it?"

"You're right. You've only scratched the surface. But you'll get the whole story. I promise."

I take another satisfying sip of wine to steel my resolve.

"I'm going after him, Ricki. I'm prepared to use all of my computer skills and every cent I have to find him. And I'm going to need somebody to watch my back — to document my story, in case something happens to me. I'm giving you the whole story, if you want it. What happened in New York, what happened in L.A., and whatever happens next, it's all going to be yours. There's just one string attached," I tell her.

Ricki swirls the wine in her cup, mulling over my proposal. She takes another sip, draining her plastic cup, then she looks me in the eyes.

"I can't write a word until you've found him," she says calmly. "Otherwise, he knows you're alive and he'll be looking for you."

"I'm sorry, Ricki. But I can't risk having him come after you if he knows you're involved. He already knows I'm alive. I sent him a message to let him know I'm watching him and I'm capable of being a danger to him. I've threatened to expose him completely if he does anything to endanger my family."

"Wow, you really are serious," Ricki answers.

"With all of his wealth and connections, I'm skeptical whether the authorities will be able to find him. But I have one big advantage they don't have. I know more about him than almost anybody, even Anika. I'm prepared to devote every hour of my day to search through cyberspace to find any evidence of his whereabouts. I know it will take time and I'll have to be patient. I have to be ready to move at a moment's notice. At first, I thought of using my old Honda Civic for the road trip, ready to hit the road on a moment's notice. Then I realized two things."

Ricki pours us both another cup of wine. She knows this conversation is going to go well into the night. "You were saying?"

"First," I continue, "I can't rely on that old car. I can't afford to have it break down at a crucial moment of the search. Second, even a new vehicle won't be much help. What if Soren travels by air? What if he leaves the continent or travels by sea? I have to be just as flexible as Soren. I'll have to travel by air, renting vehicles and living out of hotels. I spent the afternoon joining major frequent flyer programs. My suitcase is packed and ready to go. All I have to do is grab my other ID's for Anna and Grace from my safe, and I'm at McCarran Airport in ten minutes."

"Other ID's?" Ricki asks. "You have more than one?"

I turn my head and gaze through my window at the surreal world of Las Vegas. I find myself thinking about how crazy my life has become since that night when I met Pastor Soren at the Gund Arena. It all seems like a blur since then — discovering Soren's real identity and motives — becoming a cybercriminal myself and having to buy two fake identities to go on the run — living on the streets of Los Angeles — and then in the floodways of Las Vegas. I laugh and smile at Ricki as I remember our chance encounter in the floodway.

"Yup. Anna Benz and Grace Wagner. But that's a story for another night. Who knows, if I don't find any traces of Soren soon, you might have the whole story sooner, rather than later."

"A girl can only hope," Ricki says, returning my smile.

I think about how quickly my world has changed in the past twenty-four hours — my encounter with Ricki Marshall and our night out at the San Remo with *The Showgirls of Illusion* — then seeing the Amber Alert on the news today.

And finally, last night's strange dream — my brain's bizarre attempt at making sense of it all. I've realized that I can't — I don't want to — keep running and hiding as somebody else. At some point, Angela Baranyi is going to have to come out of hiding — exposing myself and becoming vulnerable if I'm ever going to reclaim my old life.

Ricki reaches out and takes my hand. I smile and give her hand a gentle squeeze, sending her a non-verbal 'thank you' for her warmth and understanding.

"I admire you, Angela. I understand why you need to do this. It's not just about finding Jonah and Soren. It's also about finding yourself, isn't it?"

I shrug, admitting silently that she's reading me like a book. We both take another slow sip of Chardonnay.

"I just want you to know that I believe in you. I see glimpses of the real you behind all your fear and your guilt. I'll be honored to watch your back on this mission of yours. You can count on me."

"That doesn't mean I'm not still scared shitless," I admit, laughing. "I guess there's a reason why everything happens. What's done is done, and I can't take anything back. But I guess the Amber Alert and seeing my portrait in that newscast were what I needed to bring me back to reality. I have a goal now, and I can see a light at the end of the tunnel. I'm going to find him and finish him for good, Ricki. If I'm lucky, and this all works out, maybe I can have my life back, and Julia and Nicholas can have a mother again."

Ricki raises her cup in salute. "To Angela. May the gods be with you and bring you back safely to Julia, Nicholas, your parents, and your friends."

I raise my cup to hers, then we drain the last of the wine from our plastic cups at the same time. We savor the moment, gazing out into the magical Las Vegas night. Neither one of us says another word. For now, it's enough for both of us to just enjoy our new friendship.

I FIND myself gazing out at the familiar twinkling of the Las Vegas skyline again, as I do almost every night in my tiny office. I've just returned from an evening out on the town with Ricki and a couple of her girlfriends. Following dinner at Batista's Hole in the Wall, Ricki and the girls took me to see Cirque du Soleil's *Zumanity* at New York, New York. Apart from my first night out to see the *Showgirls of Illusion* with Ricki, this was my first night out in public in two years. It was the first time I've been able to be relax and be myself in a public place, and allow myself to laugh hysterically with Ricki and the other girls.

My introduction to Cirque du Soleil was inspiring. The artistry, grace, and strength of the gymnasts created a visual feast for the eyes, as did the sensual choreography and suggestive costumes of the performers. I'm surprised that it left me feeling so aroused again, just as the *Showgirls of Illusion* did a few nights previously.

All of the friendly banter during dinner and after *Zumanity* definitely made me curious. Ricki's two girlfriends raved about the physiques of both the male and female performers in the show. They made all kinds of lewd suggestions about the kinds of sexual positions at which each performer might excel. On the other hand, Ricki didn't say much. But I sense a masculine side of Ricki that I didn't notice during our first night out.

I wonder if she's gay? I couldn't get a good read on the other two. They both seemed turned on by the men — but then again, they seemed just as enthusiastic about the female performers. Bisexual? Oh well, it doesn't matter to me. They made me laugh and I enjoyed their company.

An alarm sounds from my laptop. It takes me by surprise because I didn't expect it to sound so soon. I move quickly to my computer table and note that my Mac's *Console* window is open. It's displaying the execution log of the Trojan virus I sent Soren. I feel a smile spread across my face. He's taken the bait.

So, my friend. Where are you? How long are you going to be online tonight? How long before I can start watching what you're doing? When will I know where you're hiding?

I hear the external hard drive attached to my Mac spinning continuously as it stores the digital bits that are now being downloaded to it over the internet.

Now for part two of my plan.

I open up my web browser and enter a search for major Detroit hospitals. The search is a long shot — my chances that the email account I'm looking for is still active is slim. The list of hospitals is discouragingly long. I set to work, systematically searching each hospital, one at a time. While I'm on the fourth hospital on the list, the alarm on my Mac sounds again.

Damn! Soren's logging off his laptop already. This might take longer than I thought.

I turn my attention back to the task at hand. I finally strike pay dirt on my seventh try — Henry Ford Hospital in downtown Detroit. The name I'm searching is still listed, along with an email address. I copy the email address and switch to my mail program. I carefully type a message to the recipient and click the *Send* button, listening to the *whoosh* of the email program as the message flies out over the internet. Seconds later, I hear the familiar *plink* of my email's Inbox.

Shit! Auto-response. He's away and won't be responding to that account. Okay, I guess I need to do a little fishing.

I go back to my browser, typing *Chateau Eden* in the search box. The nudist resort's website pops up in my browser and I go right to the *Contact Us* page and type a message:

Hello.

I understand from TV news reports that Dan Whitney is currently living at your hotel. Please tell him that both he and Francesca have seen me, but don't know me. Please understand that I can't reveal my identity right now. I am in great danger, as is Francesca, Dan, and his friend, Anika. I am also searching for Soren Kristiansen. Please believe me when I say I am Dan's friend. I will soon be able to watch over him from a distance and warn him of

any dangers from Soren. Please pass this message along to Dan or Francesca as soon as possible.
  Your Guardian Angel

I press the *Submit* button on the website and send my inquiry to Chateau Eden. I smile, knowing that my message will be sure to grab Dan's attention. Satisfied with the night's accomplishments, I go to my bar fridge and open a small hotel-sized bottle of California Malbec with a screw-top lid. I pour it into a plastic wine glass, then wander back to the wall of windows at the front of my office.

I gaze out at the sparkling cityscape with a renewed sense of hope. Things are starting to fall into place. The hunt will soon begin, and I'll be taking my first step toward venturing back out into the world to reclaim my life.

MY EYES flutter open as my apartment's ancient air conditioning groans and rattles to life. I tilt my head for a look at my clock. It's eleven-fifty on Wednesday morning. The second-floor office is already starting to feel the effects of the unforgiving rays of desert sun. I swing my legs over the side of my pull-out couch, yawn, and stretch my arms. Heaving a big sigh, I lean down and scoop my panties and bra off the floor, digging deep for the motivation to get through another long day. I'm still waiting for a sign that I've completed the hack into Soren's computer.

It's been a week since I sent the email to Soren. I'm aware that I'm having more and more difficulty motivating myself with each passing day, while I wait for another message from Soren's laptop. I know I'm sinking back into a depression, but I feel powerless to stop the downward emotional vortex. I shuffle over to the TV and click it on.

'... *temperatures in the valley today will creep close to the one-hundred-degree mark for the first time this year, as a high pressure system moves into place over most of the American Southwest...*'

"More of the same, just hotter," I say to myself, as I shuffle my naked body over to the desk, then automatically flip open the lid to my laptop. I glanced idly at the control panel window for a progress report on the synchronization with Soren's computer. Robotically, as I've done each morning for the past week, I turn to walk away from the machine, carrying my worn panties and bra in her hand.

I really need to go out to buy new undies. Someday.

Suddenly, I stop dead in my tracks. My eyes dart back to the screen. I stare at the control panel and blink my eyes.

Synchronization Complete.

It takes a few seconds for the words to sink in before I drop the undergarments to the floor, pull my rolling chair up in front of the computer, and sit my naked body down in front of the screen. I begin typing commands in the control window.

Where the hell are you hiding, Soren?

My fingers stop typing and I wait while my machine starts tracing the connection between our two computers. The seconds tick by, seeming like minutes. As the length of time increases, I start to smile.

So, that's the way you're playing — you're re-routing yourself through multiple servers around the world.

My fingers go to work again, typing in commands to modify the search parameters in my control panel. Progress is painstakingly slow, and I realize it will be more difficult to pinpoint Soren's exact whereabouts. My computer will keep fine-tuning its search to narrow in on his whereabouts.

While the machine works away silently in the background, I skip my nude body over to the office's tiny closet, suddenly finding myself energized. I quickly pull on a pair of clean panties and a fresh bra, then a pair of capris and a clean tank top. I rush back to the desk.

Unable to pinpoint IP Address: Nearest approximation — Australia.

"Yes! Australia!" I shout aloud, pumping my arm in celebration. My mind, now fully alert, starts running through the ramifications of this new piece of information.

Watch out, Soren. I'm coming to find you!

My thoughts are racing out of control. I'm trying to think of everything all at once. Instinctively, I take a deep breath and let it out in a long sigh. Gradually, the thoughts slow down and I manage to regain control.

Okay, Angela. You've got to get your butt down under as fast as possible. It will be easier to pinpoint his location once you're there!

My fingers and my mouse jump into action. I start to search for a seat on tomorrow night's flight from Los Angeles to Sydney.

"Shit!" I mutter. "I need a freakin' visa?" I huff in frustration. Once again my fingers go into action, bringing up the website for the Australian government. I set to work, completing the online application form. Abruptly, I push back my chair, leaping across the room to a counter beside my closet, grabbing my purse and leaping back to my chair in one fluid motion. Rummaging through my purse, I finally find my wallet. Flipping it open, I withdraw the Visa credit card bearing Anna Benz's name. My fingers fly over the keys, paying the exorbitant expedited fee and completing my application. I hit the *Return* key.

I feel my heart pounding. I realize that I've been holding my breath while typing my credit card information. In the last half hour, my sluggish brain has surged back into high gear. I feel a flood of mixed emotions racing through me — excitement that is fueling me with renewed motivation and energy — frustration at having to wait for the Australian visa before I can begin the physical hunt for Soren — anxious anticipation of becoming a chameleon and putting my Anna Benz identity to work. But most of all, my mind is leaping ahead in time, dreaming of what it will be like to walk up to the front door of my parents' small house in Cleveland, and to take Julia and Nicholas into my arms again.

I jerk my mind back to reality, refocusing my attention on the clone's control panel. My fingers type out another command. The prompt blinks rhythmically for a few seconds. Suddenly, a large new window opens on my computer's desktop. I feel a huge sigh escaping slowly from my lungs as the reality of what I'm viewing sinks in — I'm staring at the mirror image of the desktop of Soren's laptop. I look at my control panel and note that the last transmission from Soren's machine was just over three hours ago. I bring up a time-zone map of the world, calculating that he must have last used his machine in the hours after midnight in Australia — early tomorrow morning Australian time.

I rise from my chair. Calmly I fill my kettle with water, flipping on the switch and hearing the appliance hiss to life. I ready my coffee mug by spooning some instant coffee into the vessel. I pour some muesli into a bowl then retrieve a container of strawberry yogurt from my tiny bar fridge. After pouring some yogurt over the muesli, I slice some fresh strawberries into the mixture and stir them together. I take the bowl over to my desk and slowly spoon breakfast into my mouth. While I chew the grains, I begin the slow, painstaking process of searching through the file structure of Soren's hard disk. My first priority is to search his email messages, hoping they'll give me some clue as to his current location. It might save me the work of having to trace his IP address. If that doesn't work out, I'll study his recent browser history.

I open Outlook on Soren's clone. He has two accounts: one for his Pastor Soren account on the WWCC server, the other a personal *Yahoo* account. My heart sinks as I search through the mailboxes for each account. There are no recent messages, either sent or received, for almost two weeks. He hasn't been using either account.

The whistling of the kettle and the click of the auto-shutoff distract me. I go to the countertop that serves as my makeshift kitchen and pour boiling water over the instant coffee. After giving it a thorough stir, I carry it back to my desk and plop myself down in the rolling chair. I take a small sip of the steaming hot fluid, then sit back and take a deep breath. It looks like it's going to be a long day.

Deep inside, I feel my motivation and determination coming back to life. I have a goal and I see a light at the end of the tunnel. I'm going undercover to find Soren Kristiansen. More importantly, I'm going to find Jonah and reunite him with his mother. And in the process, I'm going to expose Soren and finish him for good. If I'm lucky, and this all works out, maybe I can have my life back, and maybe Julia and Nicholas can have their mother again.

Game on, Soren — who's chasing who now? Let's see which one of us is best at hiding like a chameleon. Don't fool yourself. You may think you can hide from me forever. But I promise I'll find you. You can't escape Angela's eyes!

THE END

ACKNOWLEDGMENTS

Once again, I would like to thank my loving wife and best friend, Peggy, for her continued love and infinite patience with my exploration into the world of writing.

I would like to extend a special thanks to Julia Gibbs for proofreading the manuscripts for *Faces* and *Angela's Eyes*, and for spotting and correcting all of the little irregularities and typos that an author inevitably fails to see. For more information about Julia, go to https://juliaproofreader.wordpress.com/.

Thanks to Jenipher for her help with the photos and cover art. And finally, thanks once again to all my friends, family, coworkers, and the other writers I've met through the social media. I thank you all for your support and positive feedback about *Walls*, and also for your encouragement while waiting so patiently for its sequel, *Faces*, and for *Angela's Eyes*. I truly hope that it was worth the long wait, and that you enjoy this novella as much as I enjoyed writing it.

Alex Jones
December, 2022

OTHER BOOKS BY

DAVID ALEX JONES

THE NIGHT CLASS
An Alternative Tale of Reconciliation

***

Originally written as Alex Jones:

WALLS:
The Survivor Trilogy, Book One

FACES:
The Survivor Trilogy, Book Two

SPIRITS:
The Survivor Trilogy, Book Three

Find out where to purchase David Alex Jones'
books
by visiting his website:
http://www.davidalexjones.com

ABOUT THE AUTHOR

David Alex Jones is a retired Clinical Psychologist who lives in Ontario, Canada. In his writing, he combines his understanding of human identity and personality, his passion for helping victims of trauma, abuse, and Post-traumatic Stress Disorder, and his love of reading fiction, to create a unique brand of psychological suspense and political commentary. His writing is rich with complex characters and controversial social issues, resulting in an abundance of internal and interpersonal conflict, dysfunction, and tension. Dave also enjoys spending time with his grandchildren, travelling with his wife, photography, and home brewing craft beer.

EXCERPT: FACES

The Survivor Trilogy: Book Two
by David Alex Jones
(Originally as Alex Jones)

A NONDESCRIPT grey mini-van made its way down Blanshard Street towards downtown. It was ten-thirty a.m. on a sunny late April day in Victoria, the picturesque capital of British Columbia. The blond-haired man behind the wheel drove cautiously, making sure to avoid doing anything that would attract attention to the vehicle.

"Are we almost there, Daddy?" asked the five-year-old boy in the back seat. A brand-new Blue Jays baseball cap covered his freshly shaved hair and cast a shadow over his face.

"Yeah, almost there," the driver mumbled. He turned to the woman seated beside him in the passenger seat. "Can you keep him quiet? All we need is for him to open his mouth and wreck everything. Do your job, Beth!"

The van made a right turn onto Bellville Street. The harbour and the Empress Hotel came into view.

"Look, Jonah," the woman said. "There's the harbour. We're almost at the ferry. Do you remember how important it is to remember our story? We don't want the bad people to catch us, do we?"

Jonah's mouth turned down at the corners, a confused look covering his face.

"Why are the bad people chasing us? Why isn't Mommy coming?" he asked.

"Shhhh!" Beth whispered. "Remember, we're pretending that I'm your mommy right now. If the man at the ferry asks you what your name is, what do you say?"

"John… John Dailey Junior," Jonah said by memory.

"And what's your dad's name?"

"His name's John Dailey too. And your name is Elizabeth Dailey. You're my mom," Jonah said.

"Excellent," the woman said. "You're going to do a good job of fooling the bad people."

"But why isn't Mommy coming with us?" Jonah repeated.

"I've already told you!" the driver shouted. "The devil has sent some very bad people who don't like Daddy's church. They don't like us spreading God's word, so they're spreading lies about Daddy and our church. If Mommy comes with us, they'll be sure to find us all. So Mommy is going to stay at home for a while. In a few days, she's going to try to run away from the bad people so she can be with us in Seattle. Now, smile and pretend that we're a happy family. We're going to visit Grandma and Grandpa, okay?"

"Okay," Jonah pouted.

Soren Kristiansen slowed the van as they approached the ferry terminal.

"You've got the passports ready?" he grunted to Beth.

"Yes, don't worry. I've got everything. Just relax."

"Don't you worry about me," Soren snorted. "Just make sure you and John Junior don't screw things up!"

Soren made another right turn onto a short road that carried them down a ramp to the Black Ball Ferry Terminal. He pulled up to the ticket booth and rolled down his window. A cheery middle-aged woman greeted him.

"How many passengers?" she asked.

"Two adults and one child," Soren answered.

"Do you have acceptable photo ID for entry into the U.S.?" the woman asked.

"Yes, we all have passports." He turned to Beth. "Do you have those passports, honey?"

Beth smiled and handed the passports to Soren.

"You'll need to show those at U.S. Immigration Pre-Clearance, just ahead. That'll be seventy-five dollars."

Soren handed the passports back to Beth and reached for his wallet, counting out a number of bills and handing them to the ticket agent.

"Thanks, sir. Have a pleasant trip."

"Thank you, ma'am. You have a nice day too," he said, flashing his warmest smile at the agent. He turned his head and looked at Jonah in the back seat.

"Okay, Jonah. This is it. All you have to do is remember that you're John Dailey Junior, and Beth here is your mom. That's easy, right?"

"Yes, Daddy."

Soren focused ahead at the security cameras, mounted on posts as the ramp descended towards U.S. Immigration. He donned his dark glasses and ball cap, making sure not to show his newly cut, very short blond hair.

"Okay then, everybody. Put on your best smiles!" he said.

Soren let his foot off the brake, allowing the van to creep along down the ramp behind a line of other vehicles, making its way towards Customs pre-clearance.

THE M.V. COHO slowed as it neared its mooring at the ferry terminal in Port Angeles, Washington. Clearing immigration pre-clearance in Victoria had gone without a hitch. The trio's crossing of the Strait of Juan de Fuca had been smooth. The almost fifty-year-old car ferry swayed gently from side to side with the small swells that rolled from west to east through the passage.

Deep inside his body, Soren felt energized by anticipation, like an athlete preparing for an important game. He was psyched. He looked at Beth and Jonah, who both looked tense. There was only one other thing that could possibly go wrong. But Anika was still at work, and she wouldn't be picking Jonah up from kindergarten for another two hours. She wouldn't even know yet that her son was gone. Soren donned his dark glasses and removed his cap, making sure his new look was captured on security video surveillance.

"Smile and relax, you two," he said. "Just make believe you're visiting Grandma and Grandpa, Jonah. Show the officer how excited you are to be in the United States. And Beth, just pretend we're really visiting your parents. Everybody ready?"

Beth and Jonah nodded in silent acknowledgment. The van was now at the head of the Immigration line. Finally, the light turned green. Soren lowered his window, allowing the vehicle to roll up to the Immigration booth. A short female agent in full body-armour, gun on her hip, greeted them with a frown on her face.

"Citizenship?" the agent demanded, craning her neck to look through Soren's open window at Beth and Jonah. Soren took the passports from Beth and handed them to the agent.

"Canadian," he answered.

"Reason for your visit?" the agent asked. She was all business, not cracking even the faintest smile.

"We're visiting my wife's parents in Seattle," Soren answered casually.

The Immigration agent scanned each of their newly acquired, forged passports, one at a time. Soren wasn't anxious. He knew the forgeries were almost perfect and the chances of detection were slim. He smiled and waited patiently. The agent was taking her sweet time. Finally, she looked through Soren's window and looked directly at Beth; then looked at the photograph on her passport.

"Your full name, ma'am?"

"Elizabeth Dailey," Beth answered.

"Your parents' address in Seattle?"

"666 West Raye Street," Beth said.

The agent looked closely at Beth's passport one last time.

"You're a Canadian citizen now?"

"Yes. I was born in Seattle, but I got my Canadian Citizenship after I married my husband. My maiden name is Andersson."

The agent leaned into Soren's window again, this time looking at Jonah.

"And what's your name, young man?" she asked.

"John Dailey Junior," he announced with pride. "But Mommy and Daddy call me John Junior."

"Do they, now," the agent said, finally cracking a faint smile at the young boy's response. She turned her attention to Soren, first looking at his shaved head, then his passport photo, which had a full head of blond hair.

"Can you remove your sunglasses, please?"

She glanced back and forth between the passport photo and Soren's exposed face.

"Anybody ever mistake you for the golfer?" she asked.

"All the time," Soren answered, laughing. "It gets tedious after a while, but what can ya do?"

This time the agent's face broke into a smile. She handed the passports back to Soren.

"I'll bet it does. Have a nice visit, folks."

"Thanks," Soren answered. "We will. Have a good day yourself."

The agent handed the passports back to Soren, who immediately donned his sunglasses. As they drove away, he raised the van's window, smiling to himself. He just cleared his first major hurdle.

He hadn't planned on running quite so soon, but Soren sensed it wouldn't be long before the authorities started looking into the church's finances. He also sensed that Anika was ready to leave him, and he couldn't let a custody battle get in the way of having Jonah. It wouldn't be the first time that trusting his intuition had saved him.

But now, it was only a matter of hours before Anika and the police would be after him. It was time to disappear.

ANIKA KRISTIANSEN rushed from her medical office. She was late for picking up Jonah from kindergarten. Her car beeped back at her as she pressed her remote to unlock it. She flung the door open, dropped into her seat, and slammed the door behind her. She grabbed her phone from her purse and tossed the bag into the passenger seat. Flipping open the phone, she dialed the kindergarten's number.

"Hello?… This is Dr. Kristiansen… I'm terribly sorry, something came up and I had to deal with it… I'm on my way now, but I'll be about ten minutes late picking up Jonah," she said hurriedly.

The female voice on the other end hesitated before answering.

"Anika?" the woman answered, confusion in her voice. "Is that you?"

"Yes, is that you, Janice? Why? Is something wrong?"

"I thought you knew. Soren picked up Jonah at ten o'clock this morning. He told me about your parents' accident. He said he was meeting you at home so you could leave for Calgary as soon as possible. I hope they weren't hurt badly!"

Anika shivered. A chill surged through her body. A feeling of dread began to descend over her. Something was terribly amiss.

"I haven't heard any details yet, Janice. I probably missed Soren's call. Things were crazy at the office. I'll call you to let you know if Jonah's going to miss some days. Thanks," she said, as she pressed the hang-up button on her phone. She dialed Soren's mobile number. It rang repeatedly and then went to voicemail.

Hello. This is Pastor Kristiansen. I'm not able to answer the phone right now. Please leave me a message and I'll call you back as soon as possible. Have a blessed day.

Anika's heart was racing. Her thoughts started racing.

I know things haven't been good between us lately, but surely he wouldn't take Jonah? Where would he go? Where would he take him? Maybe he's at home!

Anika dialed their home number, praying that Soren would answer. With each ring, she felt her heart pounding harder. When the call went through to voicemail, she hung up and tossed her phone in the passenger seat. She fastened her seatbelt, turned the key in the ignition, and slammed the vehicle into reverse. As she backed out of her parking spot, she sensed a blur in her peripheral vision and slammed on her brakes. The other car screeched to a halt, blaring its horn at Anika. The man behind the wheel flipped her the bird, then drove on.

Anika took a couple of deep breaths, let her foot off the brake slowly, and then backed the rest of the way out of her parking spot. She jammed the vehicle into *Drive* and her SUV flew out of the parking lot, tires squealing as she turned right onto Blanshard. She headed for the highway back toward Brentwood Bay.

Rush hour traffic was heavy on the highway. It seemed to take forever to reach the Brentwood Bay turn-off. Anika's mind raced and her hands were locked onto the steering wheel as she sped along Mt. Newton Cross Road. Two more turns, and she came to their cul de sac. Anika swung into the driveway, slammed on the brakes, threw the transmission into *Park*, and flung the driver's door open, all in one motion. Her hands shook and she fumbled impatiently with her keys, trying desperately to open the front door to her home.

Finally, her key seated in the lock and she turned the deadbolt. She threw the heavy door open.

"Jonah! Soren! Anybody home?" she screamed.

Anika was greeted by an ominous calm. Except for the steady ticking of the grandfather clock in the hallway, the house was silent. Anika's heart pounded. Her chest was tight and she struggled to catch her breath.

"Jonah," she whimpered. The clock ticked relentlessly and Anika's heart sank. Reality started to set in. She ran upstairs and then down the hallway to her bedroom. Her jaw dropped when she threw open the door. Soren's closet door was agape. His bureau drawers were hanging open. He'd clearly gathered up some clothes and left in a hurry. Anika ran to Jonah's room and was greeted by the same sight.

With a growing sense of dread, Anika marched down the hallway, down the staircase to the main floor, then downstairs to the basement. The basement light was already on. Her eyes were drawn to a glaring gap on their storage shelves where two suitcases had been stored. Her mind was now spinning out of control. She began to feel violated—worse than if somebody had put a knife to her throat and threatened her life—she felt angry and betrayed. Then the floodgates opened and she became overwhelmed by a flood of emotions— anger, betrayal, fear, helplessness, sadness, loneliness and guilt. But most of all, it was anger that raged inside her.

Anika felt like there was an anvil on her chest, preventing her lungs from sucking in any air. She dropped to her knees on the concrete floor, gasping for breath. Tears filled her eyes.

She sobbed inconsolably while she struggled to breathe. Time seemed to stand still. She had no idea how long she spent on her knees. Gradually, she felt the pressure easing off of her chest. Her knees throbbed. She managed to hoist herself to her feet and slowly ascended the stairs, first to the main floor, then to the upper floor. She wandered into Jonah's bedroom and sat on his bed, reaching for his favourite stuffed animal; a tattered and worn panda that Anika's parents had given him for his first birthday. She pulled it close to her body, and then curled up on the bed. Her sobbing didn't stop until she had cried herself to sleep.

* * *

EXCERPT: WALLS

The Survivor Trilogy: Book Three
by David Alex Jones
(Originally as Alex Jones)

FROM BEHIND THE WALLS she had erected in her mind, Francesca Capellini struggled to comprehend last night's real-life nightmare.

As though she was on autopilot, her lean, naked, 41-year-old body had been swimming mechanically, back and forth, through the cool cleansing salt water of the swimming pool for the past forty-five minutes. As she swam, her mind battled within itself to try to understand, but also to forget, the terror of last night.

The sun was low in the eastern sky, just beginning its ascent over the California desert and the isolated estate, high in the hills over Palm Desert, where Francesca and her husband, Philippe, lived their reclusive, luxurious lives.

She struggled to stay in the moment, and to keep herself focused on the calming sensations of the water flowing over her skin.

Her efforts to keep her mind present were in vain. It drifted back to her youth in Manarola, Italy. In those days, she had learned to find escape from the loneliness of her home, and from the shame of the sexual advances and humiliation of her older sister's husband, Paolo. Rising at dawn, stripping off her clothing, and swimming in the Mediterranean off the rocks surrounding the village's small marina, it was the one place where she felt free and could cleanse herself of the shame that seemed to cling to her after he had humiliated her or used her young body.

The memories of those dark times from her past began overwhelming her brain. Walls came up in her mind to block them, but it was too late. Those haunting memories from her past connected with images and sounds from the surreal events of the last few hours. The sensory overload of those old memories, plus the nightmare of the past few hours, was working its way up and over her walls, creeping into her consciousness. She saw ghostly images of the young Columbian man shouting at Philippe and heard distant screams of anger from Philippe in reply. Then there was the anguish and fear she'd heard in the young woman's cries. It was as if she was living it all over again. The images, screams, and cries from last night flooded into her consciousness as she swam.

Francesca felt cold fear course through her body. Her muscles tensed, her heart pounded, and her strokes became more labored.

Then, there was only darkness.

In her mind, Francesca felt the cold desert air of the February night chilling her to the bone. Her muscles were trembling, but she couldn't tell whether it was from fear or the cold. She was vaguely aware of sitting in the passenger seat of a car in the darkness.

In the distance, she heard a seemingly endless cycle of sounds: a shovel sinking into the gravel, occasionally striking a stone, a human grunt, then a brief pause before debris could be heard hitting the ground nearby in the darkness. The rhythm repeated itself until she had no sense of time.

Suddenly, the shoveling stopped and the implement dropped to the ground.

A voice with a heavy French accent barked out of the darkness in frustration.

"Are you going to help, or must I do everything myself?"

Francesca forced herself out of the car and moved reluctantly around to the trunk, where Philippe waited impatiently.

"Lift his legs!" he commanded.

Philippe grabbed the man's upper body. As Francesca's arms circled a pair of rigid legs, she caught a glimpse of the victim's lifeless white face. She gasped, her lungs and her legs momentarily paralyzed as she stared at the ghost-like visage.

Philippe tugged on the body. Francesca's legs and lungs jumped back to life. She struggled with the lifeless weight, doing her best to look away at the ground as they staggered towards the shallow pit in the desert floor.

There was a dull thud as the man's body slid out of her frozen hands and dropped into the makeshift grave. It was all she could do to keep from vomiting as she forced herself to repeat the same repulsive process with the young woman's corpse.

Francesca's body continued swimming on autopilot. She felt filthy and nauseated, trying desperately to refocus her mind on her swimming, and to bring it back into the present. As she glided out of the shadows and into a sunlit area of the pool, the brilliant morning sun blinded her, bringing her body and mind out of the darkness simultaneously.

Where did Philippe say he was going?

One part of her identity vaguely remembered them showering to remove all traces of the grime, sweat, and evidence after returning from the desert just before sunrise. Philippe was agitated as he followed her out to the pool afterwards. He was incoherent, and rambled on about having to go to Tijuana to dispose of the South American couple's rental car.

Then he abruptly left her alone, and Francesca started swimming.

As she swam, her mind escaped to Manarola, to the memories of swimming along the coastline of northwestern Italy. In her mind, she was rolling over and floating on her back. She felt as if she was twelve years old. The buoyant Mediterranean waters kept her afloat as she gazed up at the azure sky and the vibrant yellow, green, and pink buildings of the town, perched on the rocky cliffs. Her gaze swept to the green terraced vineyards that carpeted the hillsides along the five-mile stretch of coastline between the five peaceful little villages that made up Cinque Terre.

Twelve-year-old Francesca rolled over onto her stomach again and continued to swim for a few more minutes in the direction of Corniglia, the next village. In her mind, she heard the laughter of dolphins playing in the distance. Suddenly, a pair of the sleek mammals breached beside her, heckling and laughing at her each time they surfaced, then swimming circles around her. She envied their freedom and their playfulness. Yet, while swimming, she felt as free as the dolphins.

Then, as quickly as they had appeared, the dolphins disappeared. In her mind, she turned around for the imaginary swim back to the rocks and the marina at Manarola. Her strokes quickened for the return swim. She was late and had to get herself dressed and ready for school.

Getting ready? For school?

Francesca's mind became confused as reality jumbled together with her childhood memories. She started to remember Philippe's ramblings, and it dawned on her that the part of her identity that was a forty-one-year-old adult had to get ready for work at the hotel today.

Philippe Morel's French accent was much thicker than usual. He was mixing French words into his English, a sign of the intense anxiety and agitation he was feeling.

"Francesca, ma chère. You must go to work as usual today. You have to be calm. You must not show any sign that anything is different. Do you understand?" he said.

"And… and tell Carmen that I have the flu. I cannot come in today. You and Carmen will manage the guests as usual," he said.

The hotel. The guests.

Francesca struggled to keep herself connected to reality. She became vaguely aware again of the rhythm of her strokes and the gentle flow of cool water caressing her skin. Both sensations were helping to calm her and bring her back gradually, bit by bit, into the present. She noticed that the yellow streaks of sunlight had spread and were bathing much of the far side of the patio in light. The air was getting warmer. She realized it was time to shower, dress, and to drive into Palm Springs to the hotel.

Francesca pushed the nightmare of the tragic murders into the dark recesses behind her walls. She coasted to the end of the pool nearest the house and pulled herself up onto the deck. Her body was covered in water droplets, causing her skin to cool rapidly. She shivered as the hairs on her arms stood upright and her nipples became firm and erect. She always felt sad to end her swims, but she also loved the feeling of the nerves in her skin coming alive. It made her feel alive.

She reached for a large bath towel and hurriedly dried her shivering body.

Pull yourself together Fran.

She was finally starting to access the businesslike part of her personality that always helped her to manage in times of stress. This was the part of her identity she liked the most. It was a part of her that her American friend and mentor, Susan, had taught her during her teen years in Cinque Terre. It was the part that helped her feel strong when the darker parts tried to take over. It was Susan who first called her Fran, and it was Fran who became the businesslike, responsible part of herself.

She started to plan what she would wear and thought about the things she needed to do when she arrived at the hotel. She was beginning to win the battle within her mind for now. As she had learned to do in her youth, she pushed those parts of herself that were feeling afraid, dirty, and ashamed back behind her walls.

Fran continued to reassure herself while she quickly showered, rinsing the salt from her skin.

Philippe is right. Just focus on your usual routine and do not worry about anything. Philippe will take care of this mess. Everything will be alright. You will see. He will take care of you. He always has.

Fran emerged from the shower, dried quickly, and hurried into the large closet to choose some cool and casual clothing. She preferred to wear more informal attire to the hotel, which she helped Philippe manage and also worked as a part time massage therapist.

She looked for something white. Something that would help her to feel clean. She settled on a simple white low-neck cotton tank top that tastefully framed her breasts and décollage. Along with the tank top, she chose a pair of white capris and a gold belt. She picked out a pair of white running shoes with gold trim that matched her belt. Once the large items were selected, she quickly grabbed some white bikini panties, a white camisole, and a sheer bra with white lace trim that went well with the low-cut tank top.

As Fran slipped into her clothes and looked at herself in the mirror, she nodded approvingly. She felt and looked crisp and clean. Professional, but still casual. Finally, she reached for a bikini and a cover-up in case is was warm enough to give massages outside on the patio.

A glance at the clock told her that she had to hurry with her hair and makeup. Fortunately, her dark Mediterranean complexion looked good without much makeup and her short black hair was easy to maintain. She hastily applied a touch of lipstick and eye shadow, then the slightest hint of her favorite Italian perfume, and she was ready to go.

Fran paused and took a single, deep breath to calm and center herself.

It worked. Her businesslike persona was ready to go. She chose a matching white purse, swiftly transferred her belongings into it, and headed for the garage.

Although Philippe insisted on addressing her as Francesca, and preferred that she dress with class and style in a way that befitted the wife of a wealthy art agent and dealer, she often longed to be less ostentatious and formal. In her choice of a personal vehicle, a silver-blue Prius, Philippe allowed her to have some input in the decision for once. But when they went out in public, Philippe would still insist that they be seen together in his luxury Mercedes or a chauffeured limo.

Fran opened the driver door and slid into the Prius, once again pausing to catch her breath. There were only a handful of places where she felt she could be herself: when she was swimming, on those rare occasions when Philippe allowed her to go out by herself with her camera, when she felt her clients losing themselves in relaxation from one of her massages, and when she was alone in her Prius, as she was now.

She turned on the vehicle and heard the soft whine of the electric motor as she silently backed out of the garage. She felt a slight vibration from the gasoline engine as she shifted it into gear and drove slowly towards the main gates of their estate.

On either side of the massive wrought iron gates, in both directions, stretched an imposing ten-foot high, stucco-covered wall topped with coiled razor wire. Philippe maintained that it was necessary to keep their estate secure from outside intruders. She knew that it could also keep people securely imprisoned inside.

Although she had some freedom to come and go, she knew that Philippe was always aware of where she went. He ensured she didn't have the resources to go far on her own. In return, Philippe had always kept her safe. Until last night.

Fran reached for the remote control to open the gates. As she did, she felt a wave of nausea growing in the pit of her stomach. Her muscles tensed, her heart raced, and her chest tightened. Once again, she struggled to control her breathing. As the Prius gradually accelerated through the opening and the gates closed behind her, she realized she was driving out into a world that was suddenly dangerous and starting to careen out of control.

* * *

274